FIRST LOVE,
LAST LOVE

FIRST LOVE, LAST LOVE

•

Elaine Shelabarger

AVALON BOOKS
NEW YORK

Published by Thomas Bouregy & Co., Inc.
160 Madison Avenue, New York, NY 10016

Library of Congress Cataloging-in-Publication Data

Shelabarger, Elaine.
    First love, last love / Elaine Shelabarger.
        p. cm.
    ISBN 978-0-8034-9935-5 (acid-free paper)
    1. Women journalists—Fiction.   2. Motion picture
actors and actresses—Fiction.   I. Title.

    PS3619.H4522F57   2009
    813'.6—dc22

                                        2008031621

PRINTED IN THE UNITED STATES OF AMERICA
ON ACID-FREE PAPER
BY HADDON CRAFTSMEN, BLOOMSBURG, PENNSYLVANIA

To my children, Debbie and Dale, with my love and gratitude for their belief in me.

And to my family and friends, both at home and abroad, for their support and encouragement.

Chapter One

Allegra sat on the terrace in the Florida sunshine, sipping black coffee and staring, entranced at the view of azure sea, palm trees, and white sand. She was home! And yet—a stranger in her own country. She had not set foot on American soil for ten whole years.

Just being here in this beautiful corner of the United States was for her the stuff of dreams. Her workaday life in England was already fading into insignificance.

She'd checked into the Cedar Bay Resort the night before, after a breathtaking drive up the west coast from Tampa, having arrived in Florida on the kind of assignment most young journalists only dream of.

Allegra had been hoping for this kind of career breakthrough ever since she had joined the staff of *Elegance,* a glossy magazine, two years ago. After getting her degree, she'd worked on a local newspaper for a year before landing a coveted job in *Elegance*'s features department. It was the kind of publication that talked to its readers in an intelligent and informed way. It combined fashion and beauty items with celebrity features and human interest stories, and it also had a strong international focus. Allegra knew this assignment was huge. And now, having arrived at her destination, it was all she could do to control the sudden attack of nerves, which dried up her mouth and turned her knees to water.

In her wildest dreams, she had never imagined meeting Max Tempest again—let alone interviewing him. It was pure chance that she had landed the assignment in the first place. She had just been about to go off on her annual leave when a senior colleague had suddenly come down with shingles. And when Helena Vane, the features editor, had asked her to step in, there was no way she could have turned it down. She'd had no elaborate holiday plans—intending to spend some time redecorating the bedroom of her tiny flat off Kensington High Street. Later, she thought she might leave the London rain behind and drive down to Cornwall to visit her brother and his young family.

"I'm sorry to ruin your holiday plans," Helena had said, "but with Carol Spencer on sick leave and others already committed, there really is no alternative. Anyway, you can stay on and spend the rest of your leave in Florida after you've done the interview. It will be a homecoming for you, won't it? So you should love every minute."

Helena was right. After Allegra's adored father died, there had been no more visits to the States. Twenty-five years ago, he met and married her English mother after a whirlwind romance while on vacation in London. Although he had made his home with her in England, he had made certain that Allegra's birth a year later had been registered as that of an American citizen. After her mother remarried, they gradually lost touch with their relatives in Colorado—something Allegra had always regretted and which she intended to rectify as soon as she possibly could.

But right now she had to contend with the squadron of butterflies fluttering in her stomach. If she'd booked her usual holiday in Spain, she wouldn't be sitting here in this particular paradise with her heart in her mouth, wondering just what she had let herself in for.

She glanced down for the hundredth time at the publicity shot of the star protruding from the bulky folder, her eyes transfixed by the dark, patrician lines of the familiar face in front of her.

"Gorgeous, isn't he?" Helena had purred. "I suppose you saw his last film? Brilliant. Absolutely riveting. No wonder he turned his back on the English stage and went off to Hollywood!"

Allegra shivered as if someone had touched an exposed nerve. Max Tempest. Alpha male. The kind whose mere presence made every other man both on the screen and in the flesh look utterly insignificant.

Max was probably the hottest box-office property to make his mark in Hollywood for years. She hadn't seen him in the flesh since she was seventeen and her flatmate Julia, who had recently landed her first walk-on part in the West End, had taken her along to a party. Max had recently arrived from the States and was in his first major role at the Globe. As a young and relatively unknown American actor, he had already begun to attract a great deal of media interest with his dark good looks and bright talent. And Allegra still went hot with embarrassment when she allowed herself to remember what a fool she'd made of herself over him.

The embarrassment of those last moments on the doorstep of his flat in Chelsea had been hard to forget.

"Go home, Allegra. Best stay out of things you don't understand!"

It had been a painful and enlightening experience, and one that she'd had no intention of sharing with her boss—or indeed anyone else.

"Make no mistake about it," Helena had said. "This is huge. It's the first time Max Tempest has ever granted anyone an in-depth interview, and he has to be handled with kid gloves. Your job is to find out exactly why he's suddenly given up his house in Beverly Hills to bury himself on a remote island—and if there's any truth to the rumor that he's made his last Hollywood film."

Allegra had flashed Helena what she hoped was a dazzlingly confident smile. Her editor, she knew, expected and got total commitment from her young-and-talented staff. When Allegra first began work at the magazine, she had spent the first few months in total awe of her new boss. It was an interview she had done with a well-known soap star that got her noticed, and from then on, Helena had taken an interest in her career. Now, having recently landed the job of her assistant, she knew that there was no way she could show anything less than a positive attitude. Like it or lump it, she would just have to get over her nerves and get on with the assignment—whatever her private feelings on the subject of Max Tempest may be.

"I'll do my best!" Allegra had said, earnestly. "It's a brilliant opportunity and I'm sure I can do it justice."

"Excellent! And as you're one of our most promising young writers, I expect a great deal of you. Of course, it won't be an easy ride. Max Tempest absolutely loathes the press. Of course"—she laughed—"if he wasn't such a lady-killer, they'd probably leave him alone. And by the way, if he sticks to his preference for blue-eyed blonds, you'd better be on your guard!"

Allegra grimaced, remembering how she'd reddened at the last remark. "Don't worry, he's way out of my league! And besides," she had added defiantly, "I'm not susceptible to his type!"

Not anymore, anyway, she thought, as she stuffed the photograph back into the folder. She'd read all the details of Max's colorful romantic life, of course. Film stars, ingénues, top models—they'd all been linked with his name. There had been a time when she'd childishly tortured herself by following it all in the tabloids. Until, that is, she'd finally grown up and put the whole crazy episode behind her. Max belonged to the past and that is where he should, with any justice, have stayed. It was just sheer coincidence that had brought them together again.

Still, she reminded herself, this was the chance of a lifetime. So what if she'd had her heart broken all that time ago? She'd moved on since then, and, in any case, there was every possibility that Max wouldn't remember the details. If he did, she'd just have to tough it out and behave like the professional she was. The fact that she knew the man had to be an advantage. He wouldn't . . . she couldn't. . . . A shiver of nervous excitement raised the fine hairs at the nape of her neck and made her skin prickle.

She groaned. She should be spending the day relaxing and preparing mentally for the interview the following day, but how could she with all this churning in her mind? She needed to do something positive straight away.

"Would you know if I could get across to Shell Island today?" she asked the friendly waitress who came to refill her coffee cup.

"Sure. Ten minutes by motorboat." Her bright, dark eyes were friendly. "But if you're a movie fan, don't bother. It's a private island and you won't ever get near Max Tempest. Even the newsmen have given up."

"So he really does live like a hermit?"

The girl shrugged. "He comes over here sometimes. Not often. Keeps to himself. We kind of leave him alone. He's entitled to his privacy, I guess."

Not for much longer, Allegra thought. Ten minutes later, she was at the marina, hiring a small boat.

It wasn't, she told herself, mere curiosity that was driving her. Since the interview was to take place at her hotel, she'd have no other opportunity to get a glimpse of Max's house. Apparently, he had lived in some splendor in Beverly Hills, and the contrast should be illuminating.

Taking a deep breath, she started the little motor, and

looking, in her scarlet vest and white shorts, much bolder than she felt, she set off across the bay.

"Did you get my e-mail, Max? Reminding you about the interview?"

The long pause, followed by a groan, would have irritated most people. But Ed Clayton had been Max Tempest's manager and mentor since the start of his film career and understood his deep distrust of the press.

"Was that an affirmative?"

"I guess so," Max grumbled, "though I still can't believe you've set me up with some pushy journalist."

"Oh, come on!" Ed grinned to himself. "It's just one short interview with a little English lady from one of those upmarket glossies. All you have to do is use your charm and she'll be putty in your hands."

"I don't do charm," Max growled. "Not with the press. You should know that by now."

"Oh, I sure do." Ed had picked up the pieces so many times lately, as a result of Max's strained relationship with the media, that he'd lost count. It was a pity that one or two bad experiences had soured his dealings with the press. "You really don't want to do the interview at your place?"

"No way! I thought I'd made it clear I don't want a journalist anywhere near this house. Particularly under the present circumstances."

"Okay, fine. We'll do it as arranged over lunch at the Cedar Bay. It's discreet, and I can rely on the manager to keep his mouth shut."

"I certainly hope so!"

"Relax, will you? It's no big deal! And hey, maybe the young lady will turn out to be hot!"

"Hot?" Max scowled. "I thought I was supposed to be convincing her what a decent guy I am."

Ed sighed. "Just kidding."

"Good! And remember, I want a time limit set. No longer than an hour. And make sure you brief her first. No personal questions."

"Sure," Ed said patiently. "Don't worry about a thing." It was a miracle that the interview was taking place at all. He'd been forced to use a mixture of cajolery and threats to get Max to agree to it. He just hoped that the journalist would handle him sensitively.

"By the way, have you made a decision yet?" Ed went on blandly. "About the new movie? That's one question she's bound to ask."

Max scowled. "And one I'm not bound to answer."

"Okay, okay. Just be pleasant and field anything difficult. Don't lose your temper. That's all I ask."

Max sighed. He knew he'd attracted bad press lately and that Ed needed him to do something about it. In fairness, Ed had no idea how much Max had come to regret his decision to leave the London stage for a career in Hollywood. Fame of this kind wasn't easy to handle, despite the wealth it brought. He'd always valued his privacy, enjoyed his own space, and at times he felt it was virtually impossible to breathe. And now, the sudden changes in his personal life made freedom from outside interference even more essential. Life wasn't just about him anymore. There was someone else to consider, someone he had to put before himself. It wasn't something he wanted to confide in Ed just yet, but he was seriously contemplating turning his back on his film career.

"I'll do my best," he said tersely. "You'd just better hope the lady behaves herself. Otherwise, I might just walk away and keep on going."

Ed grinned as he hung up. It hadn't been easy to pin the elusive star down, but now the die was cast and Max would just have to get on with it.

Allegra stood at the water's edge on the deserted beach. So this was Shell Island. The tiny crescent of white sand, protected on both sides by outcroppings of pink rock and backed by palm trees and towering pines, was even more picturesque than she had imagined. And from where she was standing, the roof of what might be Max Tempest's island retreat was just visible through the trees.

There was a knot of anxiety in the pit of her stomach as she dragged the little boat over the sugary sand above the waterline—an uneasy feeling of foreboding she couldn't quite ignore. She prayed her presence wasn't being picked up by some security camera. She couldn't afford to mess up. The last thing she needed was to antagonize Max. In fact, she reminded herself as she made her way up the crumbling stone steps over-hung with pine and fir, the last thing she needed at the moment was Max. Period.

"Where exactly do you think you're going?" The deep male voice sounded distinctly hostile.

Allegra, clinging for dear life to the seven-foot boundary wall and about to throw her leg over the top, froze.

All the conventional things that happened to trespassers caught in the act engulfed her. Her heart began to thud against her ribs, her mouth dried up, and small sharp prickles of adrenaline spiked through her veins. Afraid to move or look around in case she lost her precarious balance, she stayed still, clinging on for dear life.

"I think you'd better get down. Right now!"

Allegra gulped. She had forgotten just how beautiful the voice was, so clear and resonant, the actor's voice that had captivated audiences all over the world. But now, with her fingers about to lose their tenuous grip on the rough white stone, this was hardly the time to dwell on such things.

"All right!" she snapped, shifting her grip. "Just hang on, will you? I'm doing my best!"

Hot with embarrassment, she gritted her teeth. She took a deep breath and jumped down, scraping her cheek against the wall as she landed and fought to keep her balance. Then, hardly aware of the pain, she turned to face the tall figure standing under the trees thirty feet or so away.

"Don't even think about running." Max Tempest jabbed a thumb at the large white-painted notice nailed to the heavy wooden doors: PRIVATE. TRESPASSERS WILL BE PROSECUTED. "Just stay right where you are."

As he reached for the cell phone in his shirt pocket, Allegra lifted her chin defiantly. "Wait! I'm not a trespasser! I'm from the magazine! I'm here to interview you."

She tugged off the dark-blue baseball cap she had bought at the marina that morning, and a cascade of bright hair spilled out over her shoulders.

Max took a step forward, one arm raised as a shield against the fierce Florida sun. "And there I was thinking you were Spiderman," he said, grinning. "You've got your dates wrong, sweetheart, as well as the time and place." His tone clashed with the term of endearment and Allegra, watching him march with characteristic grace and speed toward her, silently cursed herself for the decision to snoop. Knowing his dislike of the press, it was the worst thing she could have done.

Wishing herself a million miles away, Allegra stood facing Max Tempest in the bright, hot circle of sunlight and forced herself to look boldly into the handsome face as she waited for recognition to dawn. He was staring at her intently, the dark brows drawn together in fierce scrutiny, and the anticipation was almost too much to bear. She colored deeply, flinching as he suddenly leaned forward and took her chin in his hand, turning her head to examine the graze on her cheek. Then all the fight went out of her, and she closed her eyes in resignation. Any second now and her humiliation would be complete.

"Not as bad as it looks," he informed her, "though it might be a little more colorful tomorrow."

He didn't recognize her!

Once she grasped that, the realization was shocking. The surge of relief she felt was quickly followed by a sharp pang of disappointment—and something else she couldn't quite identify—but somehow she managed to disguise her reaction.

"It's just a graze." She stepped away from him quickly. "Look, I know I had a nerve coming here. I just wanted to get a quick look at your house. As background for the article." She attempted a jaunty grin. "I didn't expect to be spotted."

"Casing the joint?" Max grinned, his teeth white and even in his tanned face.

"Just looking. If you'll accept my apologies," she said hopefully and made as if to go past, "I'll make myself scarce until tomorrow."

"Just a second." Max reached out a square, powerful hand and took her arm, and the touch of hard cool fingers against her hot skin sent a spasm of sensation along her nerve endings. "You owe me a better explanation than that. You crazy journalists will do anything to get a story. It's obvious you're here for a reason. You might as well come clean."

Allegra shot him a look of cold disdain. The fact that he hadn't recognized her was insulting enough. But his cynical attitude was the last straw. She shook off his restraining hand.

"Oh, please! Spare me all this macho posturing. I've told you why I'm here."

He was studying her critically, still with that air of arrogance that had always seemed to come naturally to him and which had made his stage presence so compelling. "Maybe I ought to get hold of your editor and let her know how keen you really are. What did you say your name was?"

Allegra looked him straight in the eye. To have spoken her own name now would have been even more embarrassing. Max had forgotten her face, but he might just remember her name. "Surely you were told you'd be interviewed by Carol Spencer," she said defiantly. "And there is absolutely no need to contact my boss."

"So how will I know you really are this person?" He raised one sardonic black eyebrow. His voice was dry, but the gray eyes were sparkling with amusement.

"I have identification, back at my hotel," Allegra snapped, praying he would not demand to see it.

"Good. You may need it. As you may already know, I'm not crazy about journalists. Especially the kind who try to invade my privacy."

Allegra looked steadily at him. He had changed very little over the years. As dark and as deeply tanned as a Florida fisherman, he was as dynamic in the flesh as he was on celluloid. The face, proud and finely drawn under the black, straight brows, was disturbingly familiar—the vividly alive gray eyes; the sensitive, mobile mouth. But the last seven years had left their mark. There were faint lines around the mouth and tiny flecks of silver in the thick black hair. Standing so close to him, it was impossible not to react to the sheer magnetism of the man, and Allegra felt with alarm the sharp tingle of nervous excitement along her skin.

"I have apologized." She tried to keep her voice flat but only succeeded in making it sound truculent. "And I won't trouble you any further."

It still stung—the fact that he hadn't recognized her. Their brief relationship had once been, for Allegra at least, such a significant episode. And clearly, it had meant so little to Max that he could not even recall her face! Suddenly, the heat felt suffocating and the sun made her feel so dizzy that she couldn't, for very much longer, sustain the effort of staring up into the dark, mocking face.

"Just a minute!" Max said in sudden alarm. He reached out and took her by the shoulders, steadying her, the pressure of his hands reassuringly firm. "You'd better come out of the sun before you keel over."

As he led her through the gate and up the steps to a wide terrace running the length of the house, Max was struggling to retain his composure. This totally unexpected encounter with the woman who was to interview him had thrown him completely. Her sheer audacity was, of course, typical of her profession, and his first impulse had been to have her forcibly removed from his property. That was before he had seen her face. One look, as she had turned to face him, had struck him with incredible force. Not just because she was beautiful with those great violet eyes and that thick fall of gold-blond hair. He'd spent most of his life in the company of beautiful women and was fully aware of the fact that beauty was only skin deep. This girl had something else—pluck and spirit and the kind of appetite for life that he had always admired.

Careful. The sudden warning voice in his head jolted him into reality. This woman was dangerous—of the breed he most despised. She clearly had her own agenda and was playing a game he didn't as yet understand. The last thing he needed was to show weakness toward someone who had the potential to cause him a great deal of trouble. That would be playing with fire.

He led her across the terrace edged by a stone balustrade and bright with flower-filled urns and seated her at the wrought-iron table beneath the striped awning. There was a tall thermos and some glasses on a tray. Max poured her some fresh lemonade, and she drained it gratefully.

"Better?" Max was finding it hard to keep his eyes off her. Despite the flushed face and air of dishevelment, she was still infinitely desirable, with her long, slim legs stretched out in front of her, a faint sheen of moisture on her satiny skin and her slender body softly outlined by the skimpy vest.

"Yes, thanks." She flinched under his keen scrutiny and put the glass down with a slightly unsteady hand. "And that was delicious."

"Some antiseptic might help that graze. I probably have it somewhere."

"Thanks, but there really is no need. It'll be fine."

He shrugged. "Whatever." He sat down opposite her. "Now, where were we?"

Allegra was trembling—the result of a potent combination: too much sun and the intimidating presence of Max Tempest. How could he sit there so composed, so calm, as if she were a complete stranger? Was he, at any second, about to realize who she was? He gave no sign of it, and the moment passed.

"First, how did you get here, anyway?" He flung himself down opposite her and poured himself a drink.

"I hired a boat," Allegra said faintly.

The ten-minute trip across the bay had been

exhilarating. With the wind in her hair and the glorious sunshine on her pale, sun-starved limbs, she had actually relaxed enough to admire the exotic beauty of the sea and the sky, blithely unaware of the kind of reception she was about to receive.

"I had no intention of making a nuisance of myself," she told Max coolly. "It was just so tempting to get a closer look at the house."

"It was?" He shook his head. "I thought my security was pretty tight. Not tight enough, by the look of it. You should have tripped the alarm. Obviously I need to get the system seen to." His eyes sparkled. "Unless, of course, you journalists come equipped with cable cutters? I wouldn't put anything past you."

Allegra took another sip of her drink, choosing to ignore the last barb. She was, after all, entirely at his mercy and palpably in the wrong. That acerbic wit of his was still operating, she thought wryly—just one of the characteristics that had made her fall so completely in love with him.

He was looking at her now with that quizzical lift of an eyebrow which made breathing difficult.

"So, Miss—er—Spencer, you're going to interrogate me tomorrow?" he drawled, managing to make the whole idea sound utterly absurd. "I'm sure you're looking forward to that?"

"Actually, not in the least." Some quality in his tone provoked her into a sudden flash of anger. "And I'm quite certain it's mutual."

His mouth twitched. "But surely you enjoy doing this sort of thing for a living? Going around the world snooping on celebrities and delving into the deep, dark secrets of their lives?"

Allegra shot him a glance of pure dislike.

"Wrong. I'm a features writer, and I wasn't originally chosen for this job. In fact, it was foisted on me because of someone's illness."

"Really? Tough call!"

Allegra mentally cringed under the long, slow scrutiny. She could not, she knew very well, have presented a very prepossessing appearance. Her sun-streaked hair hung around her face in damp ringlets. Her face was wet with perspiration from the hot scramble through the trees. Her arms and legs had begun to turn pink, and the sea-spray had reduced her white shorts to a crumpled mess. As the appraising eyes swept over her, she was gripped once again with the fear that he might suddenly somehow "place" her, but there was, thankfully, no sign of recognition.

"So," he went on, his voice ironic, "I shouldn't flatter myself that you're here because you're a devoted fan?"

She refused to be drawn. "Naturally, I've seen your films. As a conscientious journalist, I always do my homework."

"I hope," he said gravely, "you didn't find it too much of a chore."

Allegra found herself struggling to keep her temper. If Helena could hear this, could see the way she was handling the wonderful Max Tempest, she'd probably have sacked her on the spot. "Establish rapport right away," she'd counseled. "Flirt with him a little! In other words, charm him!"

Some hope, even if she'd wanted to—which, of course, she didn't.

She stole a look at him, at the way, even lounging in a garden chair, he managed to look as if he was playing the romantic lead in an epic film. He was wearing threadbare blue Levis and a soft white shirt open at the neck to reveal the strong brown pillar of his throat. The whole impression was one of powerful, intimidating masculinity that would have made him, even without the trappings of stardom, conspicuous anywhere.

Allegra steadied herself—the way things were going, she'd shortly find herself out on her ear and the interview canceled. She had a job to do, regardless of her personal feelings, and it was high time she got on with it.

"Look," she said in what she hoped was a sweetly reasonable voice, "we seem to have gotten off on the wrong foot. And it's entirely my fault. I had no right to intrude in the first place."

"Correct." He suddenly gave her a lopsided grin, which for years had left women of all ages swooning in the aisles.

"I really am sorry." Allegra swallowed hard. "Am I forgiven? And may we start afresh tomorrow?"

"I guess so." He shrugged the broad shoulders. "We seem to be stuck with each other, Miss Spencer, so we might as well go through with it. Maybe our meeting tomorrow will be a little less bizarre than today's."

Allegra took another steadying breath, determined not to be drawn. "I assure you it will be. I gather you don't normally give interviews of this kind."

"You're right." His mouth quirked sardonically. "If I

could have avoided this sort of nonsense, believe me, I would have."

"I understand. Well, I promise not to take up too much of your time."

He gave her an amused glance. "No chance of that. Once you've got enough to fill up a couple of columns of purple prose, we call it a day."

"I'm not a hack!" Allegra retorted. "I actually write quite a wide variety of articles. General interest, mainly—social issues, politics, the arts."

"Theater and film?" He looked interested.

"I'm not an expert in that field."

"So I needn't expect you to savage my next film when you review it?"

"You're quite safe." She smiled. "I'm not a critic."

It was time, she felt, to make an exit. What was that phrase of her father's? Quit while you're ahead! But as she stood up, she was horrified to find that she was still trembling and that her earlier dizziness had increased.

"Thanks for the drink." She heard her voice as if from some distance. "I'll make my way back to the beach now."

Her voice trailed off as she turned, and the movement was too fast. There was a strange, tight sensation in her head, and the ground under her feet suddenly tilted.

Then, as she fumbled for the back of her chair, Max was on his feet, his hands on her shoulders.

"Hold on!" His voice was urgent. "Don't go fainting on me!"

Chapter Two

The rushing noise in Allegra's ears grew louder as the world suddenly moved sideways. She was dimly aware of being carried across the terrace while her head seemed to be spinning like a kaleidoscope. She had a vague impression of coolness, and as she fought to hold back the darkness threatening to engulf her, she felt her body relax against soft leather and then the cold rim of a glass thrust against her lips. Raw spirit burned in the back of her throat and made her cough. Normally she hated the taste of brandy, but now the sour sting of it on her tongue was comfort.

Max, kneeling at her side with one hand supporting her head and the other holding the glass, watched the arc of her eyelashes fluttering against her cheeks and saw the tiny pulse beating fast at the base of her throat. Lying there, stripped of her defenses—her vulnerability was disarming.

Then, as she tried to sit up, pushing the glass away, his mind struggled to shut down the feelings she evoked.

"Just relax!" he told her. "You'll do fine."

The deep voice was infinitely soothing. Like being caressed, Allegra thought confusedly, by a velvet glove.

Then common sense reasserted itself.

"I'm all right," she murmured in a sudden panic, and tried to struggle to a sitting position. But Max's strong hands were restraining her.

"For Pete's sake! Take it easy!" His face was so close to hers that she caught the scent of expensive cologne and felt his breath warm on her cheek. "Just lie still for a few minutes!"

Allegra obeyed unwillingly, conscious that her heart was beating uncomfortably fast, and forced herself to concentrate hard on her surroundings. The room he had brought her to was long, low-ceilinged, with white walls hung with boldly exotic modern paintings. One entire wall was of glass, screened against the morning sun by slatted wooden blinds; another was lined with books; and the floor was of pale wood, softened here and there by thick rugs in muted colors. The room was sparsely furnished—a couple of deep sofas and two armchairs in soft hide and some low, white tables holding heavy lamps made of Mexican pottery. An expensive room, Allegra thought—but its beauty came from the simplicity of its design, with none of the ostentation one would expect in the home of a Hollywood superstar.

Max let her sit up when the color began to return to her cheeks, and looked at her critically.

"It's the sun," she informed him shakily, running a

nervous hand over her disheveled hair. "And I suppose I'm a bit jet-lagged. I arrived late last night, and I couldn't face breakfast this morning."

"Not very intelligent, was it?" The gray eyes were mocking. "I suppose I should be flattered that you couldn't wait to get started on me."

"We've been into all that," Allegra said doggedly. "And I'm feeling perfectly fine now. I really mustn't take up any more of your time."

"I'm afraid you must. I don't make a habit of offering journalists lunch, but I guess I'm about to make an exception."

"Absolutely not!" Horrified, Allegra struggled to her feet, and then, still light-headed, sat down again quite suddenly. "I mean, no, thank you! There really is no need."

"Unfortunately, there is. Besides"—his mouth twisted in amusement as he got to his feet—"I would hate you to inform your readers that I was inhospitable."

Allegra felt panic rising. This was far more than she had bargained for and it served her right. She had backed herself into a corner and had no hope of extricating herself.

"I couldn't possibly," she began, then stopped. Was she crazy? What self-respecting journalist would pass up the chance to have lunch with an A-list celebrity? She looked up, startled, as the door across the room opened and a small figure wearing a yellow T-shirt and shorts stood on the threshold.

Enormous sea-blue eyes fringed with thick black

lashes regarded Allegra curiously before the boy switched his gaze to Max.

"You're back early," Max said, the expression on his face quite unreadable. Then he looked at Allegra. "Miss Spencer," he said, "this is my nephew, Jack."

Having pointed his guest in the direction of the cloak-room, Max stood for a few moments, looking down rue-fully at the small boy at his side. It was just sheer bad luck that the housekeeper had decided to cut short her trip to Cedar Bay and brought him back early. He should not have succumbed to the sudden desire to extend the visit of his unexpected guest. If he'd sent her packing as he should have done at the outset, she would never have laid eyes on Jack.

"What happened?" he asked him. "Did you give Maria a hard time? Weren't you having fun?"

Jack shrugged and gave his uncle a look that said it all. He was fond of Carlos's wife, but how much fun could a small boy have on a shopping trip with a middle-aged lady?

Max put out a hand and ruffled the boy's dark head. He wasn't handling this new role too well. It was diffi-cult to know how to keep a small boy amused and en-tertained when he'd had zero experience with kids. He should perhaps have hired a nanny. The idea of a com-plete stranger living under his roof was anathema to him, but he might have to consider the possibility in the future.

"I'm sorry, bud," he said. "We'll go fishing tomorrow."

"Promise?" The small face lit up.

"Sure. Right after I've done the interview with the journalist."

"You mean with that lady? She's pretty."

"Yes, she is."

Pretty or not, he thought grimly, he would have to make it absolutely clear to his unexpected guest that Jack's presence here was not something he wanted advertised. Unless he had those assurances, the interview would simply not go on. He was tempted to ring Ed for advice. But then, he reminded himself, he was pretty sure his wishes would be respected. He was not, after all, dealing with some predatory newshound out to cause trouble!

Allegra stood barefoot on the deliciously cold marble tiles in the cloakroom and sluiced water over her burning face. It had been quite a morning. First, the shock of being caught trespassing, then the humiliation of not being recognized. Not that she was surprised by that. After all, people changed in seven years, and Max, she told herself acidly, had probably forgotten many more memorable faces than her own. As if all that wasn't bad enough, she'd had to embarrass herself further by almost passing out. No wonder the casual introduction to the small boy had almost gone over her head. It had all been too much to take in the space of a single morning. She'd had no idea that he had a nephew—or even a brother or sister, come to that—but then, why would she? It was probably one of the best-kept secrets in the movie industry.

As she attempted to repair the damage done by sun

and sea, she felt suddenly grateful that she was no longer the naïve child Max Tempest had known all that time ago. What a child she had been when she had first fallen under Max's sophisticated spell, a child trying to break into an adult world—the kind of brittle, artificial world that had once seemed so glamorous and which, these days, left her cold.

She stared at herself critically in the mirror. The faint bruise was just beginning to color, and the graze, though superficial, looked sore. She had burned across the cheekbones, and her eyes were feverishly bright. She wasn't looking her best, to say the least! Perhaps it was just as well that Max hadn't recognized her! But had she changed emotionally as well as physically in seven years? Was she deluding herself that she was well and truly over him? Hadn't this awkward contact with him reawakened feelings she would prefer to forget? As she ran a comb through her hair she resolved to deal firmly with those terrifyingly familiar sensations. She would begin by letting the past go and concentrating on the here and now.

Applying lip gloss with a slightly unsteady hand, she searched for something cool and soothing for her taut skin. The row of toiletries on the shelf was uncompromisingly male. In fact, she thought, this was the hallmark of the entire house. Put together with exquisite taste and obvious expense, it ostentatiously belonged to a man. The luxurious modern furnishings were strictly functional, and nothing Allegra had seen so far showed evidence of a woman's touch. And it was definitely not the sort of house a child would feel comfortable in.

Perhaps she would learn more about Jack at lunch, and if that was the case, she reminded herself defiantly, she'd have a real scoop on her hands. Helena would be delirious.

On that thought, Allegra took one last despairing look at the blond, sun-bleached image in the mirror and then went to face the ordeal of lunch.

The small boy waiting patiently for her in the hall wore an expression of undisguised curiosity.

"Do you live in England?"

Allegra smiled. "Yes. In London."

"Cool! Have you met Queen Elizabeth?"

"No. But I've been close to her once or twice."

"Was she wearing her crown?"

"No. You see, she only wears it on special occasions."

"Really?" Jack looked unimpressed.

He considered her for a moment. "Are you really going to write a story about Max?"

Allegra smiled. "I'm going to try."

There was a distinct likeness between uncle and nephew, she thought. The hair as glossy and dark as Max's, the same straight brows and large, expressive eyes.

"Will I be in the story?" he asked.

That, Allegra thought, was the $64,000 question.

"Maybe."

He nodded gravely and it came to her that he was, in his own small way, as poised and self-assured as his uncle. His manners were excellent, and he was clearly quite used to being in adult company.

She followed the small figure across the square hall with its polished terra-cotta floor. The stark white walls were hung with exquisite paintings, and Allegra thought the David Hockney nearest the window was probably an original. She would love to have lingered there, but Jack had opened a door on his left and was standing politely aside for Allegra to enter the room.

"At last!" Max, waiting for them in the dining room overlooking the sea, shot her an appraising glance. "I was beginning to think you'd managed to escape."

"I gave it some thought," she shot back as she crossed the room.

One end of the long glass-topped table was laid, Allegra noted, for three, with snowy linen and heavy silver cutlery. A smiling, dark-haired man wearing a white jacket was hovering near a laden trolley.

"This is Carlos," Max said. "He and his wife, Maria, keep me in order."

Carlos grinned. "We try our best! Sometimes"—he shrugged, his black eyes mischievous—"it can be difficult, you understand."

Allegra, laughing, let him seat her opposite Max, conscious of his eyes on her face.

"Looks as if you've burned a little, Miss Spencer." He grinned. "The wages of sin, maybe? These little reconnaissance trips can sometimes get you into all sorts of trouble."

"Nothing I can't handle." Allegra gave him a defiant little smile. She was not enjoying this awkward, formal little meal—she felt like an intruder—but she had to admit that she was absolutely ravenous.

The food was simple but beautifully cooked and served. A salad with a piquant dressing and scallops served in the shell, lightly flavored with herbs. She accepted a glass of perfectly chilled Chablis, which perfectly complemented the meal, and Allegra began to feel less nervous.

"How old are you, Jack?" she asked him.

"Seven."

Allegra looked at the small boy's serious little face. There was an air of gravity about him that she found intriguing.

"It must be amazing—living in Florida," she went on smoothly.

Jack looked wistful. "Sure—but I live in New York."

Allegra glanced up to find Max's eyes on her. He knew she was speculating and had somehow read her thoughts. There was another taut silence while Carlos removed the plates. He bent and whispered something in Jack's ear, and the little boy grinned, shaking his head.

"The little one, he eats like a bird." Carlos gave Max a fierce glance.

"He'll eat when he's hungry." Max shrugged.

The little man went off muttering, clearly far from pleased, and then brought dessert—a bowl of exotic fruit and some English cheese. He set a dish of ice cream down in front of Jack and gave the boy a gentle pat on his head.

"No lunch. No beach. Okay?"

Jack glanced up quickly as if to see if Max agreed and picked up his spoon when he nodded.

"D'you like swimming?" he asked Allegra.

"Yes, I do. Especially in the sea."

Jack nodded. "Me too. And when Max has time, he's going to teach me to sail a boat." He scraped the last of the ice cream out of his dish. "Can I get down now?"

"Sure." Max nodded. "While you're waiting for Carlos, you could try that new computer game I got you."

Allegra watched the little figure leave the room. "Jack is very . . . mature for his age."

Max nodded. "He's a quite a character. But I think he's kind of bored here. Used to being with other children, I guess."

For the first time, Allegra noticed he looked ruffled, as if talking about the boy made him uncomfortable.

"I don't know a damn thing about kids," he growled. "Jack has been raised up north. I haven't been around him much."

"And this is his first visit to Florida?" Allegra knew she was pushing her luck.

Max shot her a penetrating glance. "Do I hear you sharpening your pencil, Miss Spencer?" he asked. "I sure hope not, because this conversation is strictly off the record."

Allegra blushed. She'd suspected that Jack's presence might be off limits—but she had not been prepared for the force of Max's reaction. "Naturally," she said, "the subject will be treated very sensitively."

"The subject, Miss Spencer, will not be treated at all." Max threw down his napkin with an impatient gesture. "If you hadn't come here snooping around my property today, you would never have set eyes on Jack. I would have made certain of that."

Allegra's jaw clenched as she fought to hang on to her temper. "Hardly snooping," she said coldly. "I'm sorry, but people like you can't expect to be invisible just when it suits you. You chose to earn your living in the public eye, so you can't have it all ways."

"That doesn't mean I have to enjoy being continually hounded!" He stared at her, a small muscle contracting at the corner of his mouth.

And then, as she braced herself for the next onslaught, he suddenly capitulated.

"Okay." He shrugged. "Maybe that was a bit strong. I'm sorry. It's just that I don't care to have my private life hashed over by the press. If the papers got wind of Jack—there'd soon be a boatload of paparazzi flashing cameras all over the place."

"I suppose so." He was right and she knew it, but by demanding her cooperation, he had placed her in a difficult situation. She had no wish to cause problems for either Jack or his uncle, but if she was to live up to the spirit of her work as a journalist, what was she to do?

"Unless I have your word that you will leave Jack out of the equation, there'll be no interview. You get that?" Max said as if he had read the conflict in her face.

Allegra shrugged. "Got it." She had no intention of pushing Max any further at the present moment. "I can understand how you feel."

"Yes. But, like you said, people like me are fair game." He leaned forward, studying her with those unfathomable eyes. "Now since this is a purely informal conversation, maybe we could change the subject from my life to yours? I'm certain I'd find it more interesting."

Allegra's heart skipped a beat. "I very much doubt it, but please—feel free."

"You're not married, I take it?" He suddenly reached out and imprisoned her left hand, examining it critically. "And no pale circle defying the suntan, I see." He smiled. "Obviously a career woman, first and last."

"Obviously." She was smiling at him quite blandly, but her stomach gave a lurch. Too many questions and she could find herself in trouble. Meanwhile, she was having difficulty freeing her hand—the hard brown fingers refused to let go.

"And will you always be content to write magazine articles—or is there naked ambition lurking beneath the very attractive surface?"

Their eyes met and held, and for a second or two, she was his captive. Then, with a strange, unnerving sensation of falling, she snatched her hand out of his grasp.

"I'd like to write something worthwhile someday."

"Such as?"

She hesitated, not sure she wanted to reveal so much of herself to him. "Perhaps," she said diffidently, "a novel. But at the moment, I'm serving my apprenticeship."

"Interesting." The gray eyes were challenging her to say more, but she refused to be drawn.

"In the meantime," she said, "I really mustn't outstay my welcome. It was kind of you to give me lunch."

If she expected him to let her go, she was, she realized, quite mistaken. He sat there smiling as she got to her feet, and the smile announced that she was, temporarily, his prisoner and that he was enjoying himself.

"Carlos will bring us coffee outside on the terrace. No, please!" he said as she tried to demur, "I insist! I believe in always doing things properly."

They sat on the terrace in the shade of the awning, drinking black Costa Rican coffee and watching the pelicans swooping low beyond the edge of the swimming pool. Allegra, staring longingly across the bay, was just able to pick out the sails of craft moored at the Cedar Bay Marina.

Seemingly impervious to her eagerness to escape, Max poured her a second cup.

"You're certainly looking a lot better, Miss . . . uh . . . Spencer. It's been quite an eventful day for you, I guess."

The patronizing note in his voice stung.

"I wish," she let out involuntarily, "you'd stop all this Miss Spencer nonsense!"

"Really?" Max gave a soft laugh. "And here I was on my best behavior and thinking you'd want to keep things formal for the interview tomorrow. After all, it wouldn't do for us to become—how shall I put it?—too intimate. It's bound to affect your objectivity."

"That won't be a problem," Allegra snapped.

"Is that right?" Max turned toward her. "I would have thought most women would find it difficult to be objective about an ex-boyfriend—however brief and unsatisfactory the experience may have been."

Allegra froze, her blue eyes widening, one hand flying to her mouth. She felt a sudden surge of adrenaline rushing through her veins, the shock of painful embarrassment quickly succeeded by a sudden flood of anger, which left her shaking, and marble-pale.

"What exactly," she hissed furiously, "are you playing at?"

Max flung his dark head back and laughed—an attractive laugh, low and spontaneous with more than a hint of mockery in it.

"I might well ask you the same question." His eyes were bright with mischief. "Did you actually believe I didn't recognize you, Allegra?"

She flinched at the sound of her name on his lips, quite unable to find her voice, her mind struggling to come to grips with the reality of the situation. So he'd known her all along! He'd been playing with her, enjoying the cruel little game, leading her on. And what a complete fool she'd made of herself!

"Oh, come on!" Max said. "What kind of an idiot do you think you're dealing with?"

Max watched the play of emotion on her face, wondering not for the first time how she could ever have imagined that he could have forgotten her. True, the elfin cap of corn-gold hair he remembered had been allowed to grow into a thick, shining mane that hung past her shoulders. But the delicate contours of her face were unchanged, although the wide-spaced eyes and full, curved mouth spoke of a confidence and poise conspicuously lacking in those early, tentative days on the threshold of womanhood.

"Why, Max?" she demanded, her voice high with repressed anger. "Why the elaborate pretense?"

"Because that's what you seemed to want." He shrugged. "So I went along with you."

"You enjoyed every minute of it!" she accused him furiously.

Max smiled, but he was already regretting the game he had played. He knew what it was all about, of course. The pretense had been a screen to cover his confusion and shock at the sight of her. He had been playing for time—a breathing space to recover. But she could have ended it at once. And he had expected her to. Instead, she had deliberately colluded with him. So what exactly was *her* game?

"I admit," he said lightly, "it was quite entertaining. But don't forget—you're the one who decided to use someone else's name. You could have come clean. So why didn't you?"

"Because," she floundered, "oh, I don't know—it just seemed . . . easier." She would not admit it had been nothing but foolish pride.

He laughed softly. "You asked for it, Allegra. Admit it."

She got to her feet, her face flushed with anger and embarrassment. "I'm glad you found it all so entertaining," she snapped. "I think I'd better leave now—before I say things I might regret."

"Not just yet." Max stood up, facing her, both amused and fascinated by the force of her reaction. "Because if you do that, I might just not feel like going through with the interview tomorrow. And then where would you be?"

"As if I care about that!" At that moment, the

interview—even her job—had faded into insignificance. All she wanted was to get as far away as possible from Max Tempest's mocking face. Over the years her obsession with him had gradually faded to a memory she didn't allow herself to dwell on. Now everything had changed. She was raw again, bruised by the cruel little game he had played, and she wished herself a million miles away.

"Think about it." He was standing very close to her, blocking her path, and she suddenly felt panic rising.

"Let me pass," she said defiantly.

The chiseled mouth curved again into a teasing grin.

Allegra thought about screaming. That would wipe the complacent smile from his face. But then what about Jack? He might hear, and she couldn't for the life of her upset the little boy. Instead, she glanced casually to her left. If she pushed hard enough, she was fairly certain Max would end up in the pool. She took a deep breath, steadying herself, but Max, reading her expression, moved first.

"Don't even think about it," he said, grinning. "Because if you try to push me in, I'll take you with me."

He took one step to close the gap between them before he reached out and took hold of her.

Instinctively, she pressed her hands against his chest to push him away, and in that moment she was lost. She felt the warmth of him beneath the thin cotton shirt, bone and muscle and smooth brown flesh; sensed his swift response to her touch; saw what was coming by the expression in his eyes. But even as she took a step backward, she knew it was too late. His mouth brushed hers, gently at first, and then, as instinct took over, his kiss deepened, piercingly sweet, and turned her knees to water.

The urge to kiss her had been so consuming, so instinctive, that nothing could have held Max back—not her look of startled surprise or the way her body had tensed, poised for flight, fluttering in his grasp like a captive bird. He caught his breath as her mouth clung to his, warm and yielding. It was a kiss that transcended the years, reminding him how long it had been since a woman had affected him so completely.

He raised his head and looked down into her face, saw that she had closed her eyes, and almost bent to kiss her again. Hang on! Where was his common sense? This was the last thing he needed. He had kissed her in a crazy moment, had completely lost his usual self-control, and was instantly regretting it. His emotional life was messy enough. He had no intention of making what could prove to be another costly mistake. He wasn't at all sure what her motivation was in turning up so suddenly, after all this time. And not quite convinced that she was telling the truth when she'd insisted she'd been a last-minute substitute for a sick colleague. It was all too plausible for his liking.

"There," he said, unsteadily, forcing a grin. "That was for old times' sake. And don't pretend you didn't enjoy it as much as I did."

Chapter Three

Allegra stepped back unsteadily, dizzy, confused, every tingling sense in her body in shrieking awareness of him. Guilty heat ran up into her cheeks. She had not expected this torrent of feeling to engulf her after all these years. She slid a shaking hand over her mouth as if to eliminate the touch of his lips and stared up at him through darkened, angry eyes.

"What was that all about?"

"Seven years is a long time between kisses." He shrugged. "I'm sorry if I offended you."

Allegra made a small, furious gesture and then checked herself. Somehow she had to hang on to her temper. The thought of Helena's anger if she blew this assignment and the inevitable damage to her career filled her, once again, with alarm.

"Look, Max," she informed him, her voice icy with disdain, "I'm not here to play games."

"Then why were you running away?"

"I wasn't running." Allegra sat down quickly, before her legs gave way under her.

"We're not strangers, after all," he said, "although you seemed more comfortable pretending we were."

Allegra shook her head stubbornly. "I don't see the point of raking up the past."

"Frightened?" He raised a dark eyebrow.

"Not in the least." She looked at him squarely. "Just not interested. I know you find that hard to believe, but I mean every word of it. I'm sorry if I've given you the wrong impression."

Max grinned. "Forgive me if I sound a trifle cynical. But you must admit, the whole situation is suggestive, to say the least. What is a man to think when he's suddenly confronted by a woman from his past who has traveled thousands of miles to see him, has ulterior motives for doing so—and whose efforts to disguise her identity wouldn't have deceived a child?"

Allegra's hands tightened on the arms of her chair until her knuckles gleamed white.

"I won't go on trying to justify my presence here," she said, striving to keep her voice calm. She'd at least gotten her breathing back to normal, and her knees had stopped shaking. "I've clearly explained once—and if that isn't satisfactory, there's nothing I can do about it. To be brutally frank, I would not have chosen this assignment. But perhaps you remember that I am half-American. I haven't had the chance to spend time here since my father died, and it means a lot to me. Also, I was the obvious choice to replace my colleague. My editor would not have taken kindly to anything but a show of enthusiasm on my part."

"And it didn't once occur to you and your editor that it might be a good idea to use the fact that you were involved with me some years ago?"

"For heaven's sake!" Allegra was almost at the end of her tether. He was so insufferably at ease, so confident and assured in his relentless questioning of her. "Do you really believe my boss would be interested in the fact that I once had a crush on you? A stupid, teenage crush?" For the first time, she sounded convincing and Max, she could see, was thrown. He stared at her, as if trying to remember her as she had once been.

"It must have been such a drag for you, Max. There I was, trailing around after you, dogging your every footstep." Allegra managed a bitter little laugh. She'd grasped the initiative for the first time and was determined not to let go. She took a gulp of her cold coffee, hoping it would steady her. "Naturally," she continued—was she beginning to ramble?—"I was young and stagestruck. And if Julia Blake hadn't invited me to that party, I'd never have done more than worship from afar."

"Julia Blake?" Max frowned in an effort to remember. "Wasn't she in the cast at the Globe that season?"

"Yes. She thought she was doing me a favor—inviting me into her world," Allegra said. "She had no idea what she was letting me in for."

Suddenly, in a heartbeat, Allegra was seventeen again, remembering with a clarity she hadn't achieved in years.

She was in her first year reading journalism at London

University and sharing a flat with Julia, three years older and fresh out of drama school, when Max first came into her life.

Julia had landed a walk-on part in a sparkling new production of *The Merchant of Venice.* To Allegra's delight, she'd wangled her a complimentary ticket for the first performance.

"Wait until you see Max Tempest as Bassanio," Julia had enthused. "He's absolutely fantastic."

She was right—one look had been enough. At twenty-six, Max was already "a name." A gold medalist at the Royal Academy of Dramatic Art, he was rapidly gaining widespread critical acclaim.

Allegra had been instantly fascinated.

For weeks after seeing him on stage, she had spent all her spare cash on visits to the theater, worshipping her idol from the distant heights of "the gods." Then one night Julia had invited her to a backstage party, and Allegra had seen Max at close quarters for the first time.

The minute she'd arrived, she was immediately conscious of him. He was standing in the middle of a noisy group, still wearing his elaborate Elizabethan costume in gold and black. But it was his presence, not just the startling good looks, that made him stand out from everyone else. His impact on Allegra was immediate and striking, and her heart began to thud with a mixture of excitement and alarm.

Someone put a glass in her hand, but she hardly noticed. Her eyes were on Max, on the dark, arrogant tilt of the head, on the handsome face, the incredible gray eyes. She could hear snatches of the conversation, and his deep voice was captivating.

"Allegra!" Julia grabbed her arm and tried to steer her away to join another group, and as she turned, she just had time to see Max look up sharply. Their eyes met for one brief, heart-stopping second.

"Amazing, isn't he?" Julia whispered with a grin. "But not in your league, so stop staring."

"Introduce me."

Incredibly, he was at her elbow.

"Oh, no you don't, Max!" Julia tried to wave him away, laughing. "Allegra happens to be my flatmate, and there's no way I'm going to abandon her to your tender mercies!"

"You don't mean that." He used his smile on her with telling effect, and Julia obediently melted away.

"Allegra." Even the way he said her name was magic.

Max took her hand and lifted it to his lips, his eyes never leaving her face, making her feel that he had been waiting for this moment all his life. And in that moment, she was entirely lost. The brief touch of his mouth made her tremble, and her heart raced. She had no idea then that she'd fallen in love. All she could feel was the powerful throb of mutual attraction—so powerful that it terrified her. She snatched her hand away as if she'd been scalded. But Max only smiled and promptly monopolized her for the rest of the evening.

Everyone else in the noisy, crowded room had faded into insignificance, and Allegra was utterly captivated, totally bewitched in a way she had never experienced before or after.

They'd sat in the wings and talked as if they had known each other all their lives: his background in the Midwest; her childhood in an English country village; his ambition, nurtured by a gifted teacher; her dreams to become a journalist.

Max was fascinated when she described her course. "Brains as well as beauty!" he had said, making her blush.

They had reached out to each other wonderingly, as if they had both discovered some rare, exquisite treasure, almost too precious to be handled.

"How old are you, Allegra?" he had asked.

The lie came automatically. "Twenty-one." She was so afraid her youth and inexperience would put him off.

In the early hours, he took her home in a taxi, and when he put his arm around her, she was lost in a heady mist of excitement and longing. He had bent and kissed her when they reached the flat—a brief, tender kiss that still managed to buckle her knees.

"I'll call you," he'd promised, as he took the key from her trembling hand to open the door. And then he was gone, and she'd walked into the flat in a trance—dazed, trembling, and utterly ecstatic.

It seemed incredible that now, seven years on, they should be sitting on a terrace in the Florida sun—intimate strangers thrown together by circumstances beyond their control.

"Can I go to the beach now with Carlos?" Jack was suddenly standing there beside them in his swimming trunks, holding a fishing net in one hand and a plastic bucket in the other. The wide blue eyes were fixed on Max's face.

"Sure. But no swimming, okay? It's a little soon after eating."

"Are you coming?" The way Jack said the words made it clear he was resigned to a refusal.

"Sure. I'm busy right now, but I'll be there as soon as I can."

"Oh, please!" Allegra, grateful beyond words for the opportunity to escape, got to her feet, grabbing her bag hastily. "Don't let me get in the way. It's all right, Jack, I was just leaving." She gave the little boy a smile and was rewarded with a wide grin.

"Go on ahead," Max instructed his nephew. "I'll join you soon."

Jack smiled at Allegra. "See ya," he said, and with a wave in her direction, he turned away and went in search of Carlos.

"Now, before you run away," Max said with a sardonic glance, "I take it you still wish to proceed with the interview. After all, it would be kind of a shame to abandon the project after all those intrepid Burglar Bill activities."

Allegra ignored the barb. "Of course. It's my job. What else would I do?"

"You won't find it a tad difficult? In view of the past, that is."

"I assure you, it won't be a problem," Allegra flared back. "Just because I once behaved like a fool doesn't mean I'm crazy enough to repeat the process."

"So I'd be kidding myself if I imagined, just a few

moments ago, that you finally decided to forgive and forget."

Allegra's eyes glittered. "Difficult as you may find it to believe, my interest in you is purely professional. And now it really is time I left." She got to her feet. "I'll see you tomorrow at the hotel."

Max nodded. "And naturally, you'll be alone. No photographers. I've already made my views clear on that."

He walked with her down the overgrown steps through the trees, and the air beneath them was humid and pine-scented. When he took her arm lightly to steady her over a crumbling step, Allegra felt her body tense instinctively, rejecting the intimate physical contact with all the strength she could muster.

He ignored her protests as he lugged the dinghy down to the water's edge and stood thigh-deep in the shallows, his wet jeans clinging like a second skin to the muscular thighs.

"Until tomorrow, then." He smiled—making it difficult to recall that five minutes ago she'd wanted to get away from him as soon as possible—and held the boat steady as Allegra, with as much dignity as she could muster, scrambled in.

Then, when the little engine roared to life, she headed the boat out toward Cedar Bay without a backward look.

Stretched out on her king-size bed in her motel room, with the air-conditioning going full blast, Allegra was finding it impossible to get to sleep.

She could hardly bear to think about her confrontation with Max that morning. He, of course, had enjoyed it all, probably convinced she was still besotted with him after all these years. He was used to women clamoring for his attention—so why should he imagine she was any different? After all, it was exactly what she had once wanted. She pressed her fingers over her mouth, and her lips tingled when she remembered the way he had kissed her. As for her reaction—there was nothing significant about that. It was just a hangover from the past, and the sooner she got her head straight and concentrated on the job she had come here to do, the better.

She lay awake for a long time. There in the darkness, images of the day crowded in on her: Her undignified descent from the boundary wall. Max's mocking smile as he pretended not to recognize her. Jack's small, serious face. She could perfectly understand the reasons for keeping his presence on the island out of the press. But a brief mention in her magazine surely couldn't do any harm. Her boss would expect it of her. The trouble was, she had mixed feelings about any kind of intrusion into Max's private life. She couldn't blame him for wanting to protect his nephew from the glare of publicity. She was devoted enough to her own nephews and nieces— if she had a child of her own, she knew she would feel equally protective.

Allegra hadn't realized how much she wanted children until Simon, the man she had shared her life with for almost a year, had made it clear that he wasn't interested in having a family.

She'd had no idea about his feelings on the subject until she'd taken him with her to Cornwall to spend the weekend with her brother and his wife and their young family. Simon, who had just passed his bar exams, had made it pretty clear that being around kids was not his favorite thing. On the way back to London, he had told her quite unequivocally that children of his own were just not on his agenda.

"You mean—not ever?"

"We're both professionals. We need to be free to get on with our careers."

It was then that she'd known that she couldn't possibly marry him—realized that her feelings for him were not the kind that that would enable them to overcome such basic differences. She had never felt as she once did at seventeen when Max Tempest had occupied her every waking thought. For him, no sacrifice would have been too great.

At first, the overwhelming emotion Max had aroused in her had rendered her deaf and blind to everything except her need to see him again. At seventeen, first love often became an obsession, overriding common sense and pride.

After their first meeting she spent hours dreaming about Max, hoping against hope that he would call her as he had promised. When he didn't, she stubbornly persisted in hanging around the back entrance of the theater, desperate for a glimpse of him. The walls of her room were covered with posters of the plays he'd been in. She coaxed his phone number from Julia and worked up the courage to phone him. But at the mere sound of the deep voice she'd been overcome with nerves and hung up with a trembling hand.

Julia was amused at first but then, wearying of Allegra's demands to repeat Max's every word backstage and describe his every movement, she'd lost patience.

"This is getting to be a joke, Allegra, and it's got to stop. Max is twenty-six and big-time. And when it comes to women, you've only got to look at him. He can take his pick. For Pete's sake, stop this nonsense and grow up."

And then just when she had given up hope, he had phoned her, quite out of the blue, and Allegra was afraid she might die of happiness. He had taken her to a small Italian restaurant where they seemed to know him, and there had only been one shadow to blight the sheer joy of being with her idol—the fact that she had lied about her age and was terrified that somehow he would find out. Max was almost ten years older and used to dating more experienced women. But she needn't have worried. When he took her home that night, his kisses were passionate, but despite his reputation, he behaved with the utmost restraint. Allegra, on her part, had never before experienced such complete happiness.

Max was totally unlike the boys she had dated—more serious, more intense, and a great deal more exciting. When the play he was in finished its London run, they explored the city together, strolling along the embankment, riding the top of a double-decker bus, wandering through the Tate Modern. Together, they marveled at the beauty of the dome of St. Paul's and watched the changing of the guard at Buckingham Palace. They took a boat down the Thames from Greenwich to Hampton Court, got lost together in the maze, and walked hand-in-hand in Hyde Park.

Allegra was in love, and a few weeks later she confided in Julia, who had been incredulous. "You can't possibly be in love with him! You hardly know him and in any case, we are talking about Max Tempest, alias the Love Rat, aren't we? You know what a flirt he is!"

"But I'm sure he feels the same!" Allegra insisted. All right, he hadn't actually mentioned the *L* word, but she was certain that would come. One day, he would go down on one knee and propose to her.

"In your dreams!" Julia said

And then just after Allegra had begun the second year of her course, she was in torment when Max called her one evening to tell her he was off to Los Angeles to do a screen test.

"I'll call you as soon as I get back," he told her.

At first she was confident that he would keep his promise, but when a whole week went by and she hadn't heard from him, she was in despair. What if he never came back? How could she bear it if she never saw him again?

Her only comfort was that Max had been invited to Julia's twenty-first birthday party and had promised to be there. Julia had hired a room at a trendy restaurant on the Thames, lots of Max's friends were coming, and Allegra forced herself to be optimistic. He would turn up! He'd promised!

She spent at least two hours getting herself ready for the moment when he would walk into the room and sweep her into his arms. She applied makeup with a lavish hand, darkening her lashes so that her indigo-blue eyes looked dramatic and luminous. When she'd added blusher and lipstick improbably named "Fiery Spice," even Julia was impressed.

"You look twenty-two, at least!"

The dress she had splurged most of her student loan on was a short, silky number in a shade of blue that matched her eyes. It clung to her slender body, emphasizing her lovely shape, floating somewhere around midthigh.

"Is it too short?" she asked Julia, tugging at the skirt rather nervously.

"Probably," said Julia cheerfully. "But you look amazing!"

"Do you really think *he* will come?"

"Max? Who cares? Forget him, Allegra! Just concentrate on having fun."

Halfway through the evening, Max walked in. He wore threadbare blue jeans and a shabby gray T-shirt, and still managed to make every other man in the room look insignificant.

Allegra froze, her eyes riveted on his face, her heart pounding. When he made his way across the crowded room toward her, she was certain her heart would actually burst with joy.

"I'm sorry I haven't been in touch," he said, hugging her. "But I didn't get back until this morning—six A.M., actually. I was bushed! Only woke up an hour ago!"

The screen test, he told her, had gone well. "There's a good chance I might land a contract with a film studio, would you believe?"

Of course she did. He was film star material—everyone knew that.

"So you'll be going back to the States?" She stared up into his face, trying to be happy for him, desperate not to let the pain she felt show in her eyes.

"If they decide they want me!" He kissed her. "Fancy coming with me?" He laughed as if he was joking, but Allegra had already made up her mind. She would go with him to the ends of the earth!

She gazed at him, lost in love, and then he suddenly frowned. "You look different tonight, Allegra! Your eyes, that stuff on your face. . . ." The gray eyes swept over her. "What have you done to yourself?"

She turned her head away in horrified confusion.

"Nothing!"

Hot color shot up into her cheeks as he took her chin in his hand and turned her face toward him.

"Just some makeup!" she muttered, and pushed his hand away. "Aren't you going to ask me to dance?"

Desperate to hide her distress, Allegra stared boldly up at him as they swayed together on the crowded dance floor.

"What is this about?" he asked her.

"What d'you mean?" she stammered. "This is a party, so I thought I'd dress up a little, that's all."

Max looked at her coldly. "It doesn't suit you. It makes you look . . . cheap!"

"Thanks!" She willed the tears in her eyes not to spill over.

The music was slow and dreamy, but Allegra moved like an automaton in Max's arms, her body stiff with pain and embarrassment.

"How old are you, Allegra?" Max suddenly stopped dancing and stared down into her stricken face.

She looked away. She couldn't go on lying. "Seventeen," she muttered.

Max stared down at her in utter disdain. "And you told me you were twenty-one. Well, great!" He shook his head. "You know something? You actually looked older without all that gunk on your face. And a lot prettier, as well."

Allegra was still fighting to keep the shameful tears at bay as he dropped his arms and stepped away from her. "Let me give you some advice," he said. "Next time a guy shows he likes you, try telling him the truth."

"I'm sorry, okay?" Allegra glared at him mutinously. "Is it really such a big deal?"

Max's eyes were like polished steel. "I don't go out with teenagers," he said.

What happened next had the quality of a very bad dream. As they stood there glaring at each other, a tall, dark-haired girl, who seemed to come from nowhere, suddenly rushed across the room and flung herself at Max.

"Max! I found you! They told me you'd be here!"

For a second, he looked utterly bemused. And then his face lit up. "Annie?" He put his arms around her and hugged her tightly. "I thought you were still in France! What are you doing here?"

"Long story!" She gazed up at him adoringly. "I so needed to see you! Can we get out of here?"

"Sure we can!"

Allegra had already turned away, afraid Max might

introduce her, not trusting herself to hide her pain. Blindly, she made her way through the noisy crowd, grabbed her raincoat, and, sick at heart, hurried out into the darkness to hail a passing cab.

It had taken her days to pull herself together. If only she hadn't dressed in that deliberately provocative way, plastered on the makeup. If only she'd been herself and told the truth from the beginning. But Max was ten years older than she was, and she was so afraid he might have lost interest if he'd known she was only seventeen! She'd been right, as it turned out, of course—but she could have spared herself a great deal of pain if she'd been honest with him at the outset. In fairness, she had always intended to level with him, but as time had gone on, her desperation to appear cool and sophisticated among the people Max mixed with had held her back. And now it was too late.

Julia, streetwise, four years older, and feet-on-the-ground, had done her best to make Allegra see sense.

"Think yourself lucky," she'd informed the tearful figure languishing in her bedroom. "I really didn't think Max was your type, anyway."

"I feel such an idiot!"

"Look, in your place, I'd probably have done the same thing myself!"

But Allegra would not be comforted. "Oh, Julia, I can't bear it. He thinks I'm a stupid child. But I know he felt something for me . . ."

"Believe me, kid, you got off lightly. He goes through girlfriends with the speed of light!"

"That dark-haired girl—Annie, he called her—was

so attractive! She looked like a model. And you could tell she adored him!"

"Probably just one of the in-crowd always hanging around him. Get over it and move on. He's not worth breaking your heart over."

Julia's advice made not the slightest difference to Allegra. She went on haunting the theater, desperate to see her idol. But when they actually came face-to-face, his nod of acknowledgment was so perfunctory that she was struck to the heart. She heard his cold, polite greeting as though it came from a long way off. She was sure she hadn't imagined the tinge of scorn in his voice.

"I hate him," she informed Julia bitterly, but quite untruthfully. "How could he walk past me like that? As if . . . as if . . ."

Julia raised her dark, expressive eyes to heaven. "If you go on like this, you'll fail your exams!"

Thankfully, she hadn't. But the memory of that last humiliating conversation, a few weeks later—with Allegra a stammering wreck and Max so remote and ill at ease—still had power to bring the color flooding to her cheeks.

She sat up, reaching for her bathrobe. Enough! She needed a long, cold shower to wash off the detritus of the whole exhausting day.

Max was on his own private trip down memory lane after watching his unexpected guest disappear across the bay. Try as he would, it was impossible to get the whole bizarre incident out of his mind. It was incredible that Allegra, of all people, should have turned up here to interview him—and furthermore, should actually imagine that he wouldn't recognize her!

True, he hadn't laid eyes on her since that winter night seven years ago. But he still regretted how insensitively he had behaved toward her. It had been his masculine pride that had made him so cruelly dismissive. He could not have admitted, even to himself, that a teenage girl had made such an impression on him that he had seriously considered giving up his dreams of stardom to stay close to her in London.

She had happened into his life at quite the wrong time, of course. His film career was about to take off, and he had his sights set on Hollywood. And then, quite out of the blue, Annie had arrived to further complicate his life.

From the moment he had set eyes on Allegra, he had known instantly that there was something more than mere physical attraction between them. He had looked across the room and met her eyes, and although they were strangers, he knew he had experienced that one perfect, unique moment of recognition. It was as if they had somehow been destined to come face-to-face.

And then that night—when he'd found out about her age. He'd been so angry—more with himself than with Allegra. Deep down, he must have realized how young and vulnerable she was. She'd made him look a fool, and his anger had made him cruel. He'd behaved like a brute.

And now? She had changed, of course, and he had been taken aback by the transformation. It was nothing to do with the way the years had confirmed that early promise of beauty. It was because that little lost look he had once found so endearing had vanished, replaced by a poise and self-assurance that proclaimed she was very much her own person—and more than equal to dealing with men like himself on level terms.

He wanted to see her again. It was as if he had been waiting all this time to finish what he had begun seven years ago. And yet he shouldn't forget that she was a member of the profession he loathed and mistrusted— or that he had no room in his life for emotional entanglements. As he went to join his nephew, he permitted himself a wry grin. His manager would never believe in a thousand years that he was actually looking forward to meeting a journalist!

Chapter Four

He was late.

Allegra, waiting in the lobby near the desk, glanced nervously at her watch. Max should have showed up ten minutes ago, and her stomach was beginning to twist itself into knots.

"May I help you, ma'am?" The young receptionist was eyeing her with interest.

"Thank you, no. I'm meeting someone."

She swallowed hard—her mouth suddenly as dry as dust. Was Max going to turn up at all? Was this the sort of stunt he liked to play with the press? Perhaps her intrusion yesterday had ruined everything. And if that was the case, she'd soon be looking for another job!

She glanced at her watch restively. The morning had dragged despite her efforts to fill in the hours browsing in the souvenir shops before the interview. The last few minutes had felt like hours!

Then, just as she was contemplating calling his agent, Max walked into the foyer flanked by two extremely dignified elderly ladies, who gazed up at him adoringly as he stopped to sign their autograph books.

Allegra smiled as she watched him chatting to them as they fluttered around him, pink-cheeked with excitement. The sight of him in such company was incongruous and at the same time strangely endearing. There was a kind of old-world courtesy in his manner toward his two admirers, which was deeply attractive. Certainly worth a mention in her article, Allegra thought with an odd little lurch of her heart. In dark-blue Levis, white shirt, and a baseball cap rammed down over his thick dark hair, he could have passed for any tourist visiting Florida. Except, she reflected, for that indefinable air of distinction about the man. It was there in the carriage of his head, in the fluid grace of his movements, as he strode across the lobby toward her.

"I'm sorry I'm late. As you see, I was waylaid!" He smiled. "Not the usual sort of fan. But irresistible."

The gray eyes swept her with a glance that brought a wave of color to her cheeks, and she was suddenly absurdly glad that she had taken extra care with her appearance that morning. She was wearing white cotton trousers and a jade-green shirt that intensified the color of her eyes. Her hair, pinned at the nape of her neck in a severe chignon, emphasized her delicate profile, and she'd managed to disguise her bruised cheek with some skillfully applied makeup. She felt that she looked well-groomed and professional—quite unlike the disheveled creature who had practically fallen at Max's feet the day before.

"Not quite a shiner." He squinted at the barely discernible bruise on her cheek.

"No thanks to you," she retorted swiftly, with a grin that took the sting out of her reply.

"It might teach you to restrain your enthusiasm for your work in future." He operated that famous smile on her, and she experienced a repetition of that breathless moment when she had turned and faced him for the first time the previous day.

Outwardly, she remained perfectly calm and collected as she felt his hand cup her elbow to lead her toward the mezzanine. Inwardly, she was floundering. Had he felt her tremble when he touched her? She really did need to get a grip.

Lunch was served in the small but beautifully appointed dining room overlooking the marina.

"Something to drink?" Max asked her as the wine waiter hovered at his elbow.

"Just water, please—no ice or lemon." She had no intention of drinking anything that might cloud her concentration. Over the simple but elegant meal of smoked salmon with linguini, she was supposed to be discovering Max's reasons for turning his back on Hollywood. The trouble was that Max, predictably, did not wish to discuss it, preferring to ask the questions rather than answer them.

"No notebook? Not even a voice recorder?" His eyes sparkled with mischief. "Maybe you're wired with a hidden microphone?"

"You've been watching too many detective movies." In her anxiety to keep the interview informal, she'd been reluctant to produce the recorder until they had finished eating. She took it from her handbag. "I'm a journalist, not an undercover cop."

He laughed. "That's comforting."

Allegra sighed, wishing that they were meeting for the first time. It would be so much easier to interview a complete stranger. But she was determined not to be sidetracked and ploughed determinedly on.

"You were nominated for an Oscar for your performance in your last film. Is it true that you have decided not to star in the sequel?"

Max shrugged. "It's a possibility."

"May I ask why?"

"Movies are all to do with money—very unpleasant stuff, don't you agree?"

"Not entirely." Allegra gave him an ironic look. Had he really forgotten those early days as a penniless young actor?

Quick to interpret her expression, he shook his head. "Let me explain that. If and when I decide to sign up for yet another Hollywood blockbuster, I become nothing more than a commodity—a piece of merchandise."

"But surely if you're not starring in the film, it will be a box-office disaster. No other actor could possibly. . . ." She stopped, hating the idea that he might think she was attempting flattery.

Max laughed. "No other actor could possibly what? Believe me, in Hollywood anything is possible. Actors like me are just cannon fodder."

"That's nonsense. False modesty doesn't suit you in the least."

"Modesty has nothing to do with it. But I'm not complaining. I had talent. I was ambitious. I wanted to make the kind of money you can't make in the British theater, so I turned my back on it and headed for the States." He shrugged. "I soon found out that making films is extremely boring. It's such a circus. There's too much garbage being made in Hollywood. In fact, the whole movie machine stinks."

"Is that why you chose to come here, to escape from it all?"

"No comment," he snapped. And then, as if he regretted his sharpness, he gave her that crooked smile that robbed the unwary of breath. "You see? I told you there were questions I wouldn't answer."

He saw her mouth tighten. She was clearly determined not to allow him to charm her into submission.

"So do you regret giving up the real theater—prostituting your art, so to speak? Even if it has made you a very rich man?" Her voice was cold, and her head came up as if bracing herself for the inevitable lash of his tongue.

She needn't have worried. He had himself well under control, and he seemed to be enjoying the verbal skirmishing.

"You really mustn't lose that temper of yours," he said. "Admittedly, it makes those blue eyes flash most attractively. But it won't get you far with this interview."

"I'll take that risk," she threw back derisively. "It was a simple enough question."

"It might have been put more tactfully."

"I'll rephrase it, then. Do you ever wish you could turn your back on all the so-called glamour and return to the classical stage?"

"Back to the theater? I don't think so." He leaned back in his chair. "Let's see, what was I doing when we met all those years ago?"

Allegra swallowed nervously.

"*The Merchant of Venice* at the Globe," she said curtly, dropping her eyes. "But as you know, I haven't come here to discuss that."

His eyes challenged her. "But surely you need to go back to the beginning of my career for the benefit of your readers?"

"Perhaps you'd let me be the judge of that," she said rather breathlessly. "I'm writing the article, and I'm actually quite familiar with the details of your career. I was just hoping for a few personal touches. Something more revealing than just a career profile."

"And how revealing would you like me to get? Are you sure we shouldn't we go back seven years or so?"

"That's totally irrelevant." The blush was fiery enough to flame her cheeks. "And I'd be grateful if you'd keep this interview strictly impersonal. That is, of course, if you have any regard for my feelings."

"If you had any regard for mine, you wouldn't have taken on this assignment in the first place."

"I'm sorry," she said stiffly. "All I need are a few quotable lines and I'm out of here. The last thing I want to do is to cause you embarrassment."

"Who said anything about embarrassment?" He

folded his arms, leaned back, and grinned infuriatingly. "Please, go ahead! This is getting to be interesting."

Max knew perfectly well that he was deliberately making things difficult. Somehow, he couldn't help himself. As the interview continued, the desire to go on provoking her was almost beyond control. He hadn't set out to give her a hard time, but some perverse need to provoke and antagonize drove him to it. He was behaving, he knew, like a small boy whose only means of attracting a girl's attention and showing how much he liked her was to pull her hair until it hurt. And he'd wanted Allegra's attention since the moment he'd laid eyes on her the previous day.

Suddenly, she'd clearly had enough. "All right, what's this about, Max? Does it make you feel good to act like a bully?"

He'd asked for it. He'd pushed her just that fraction too far, and now, looking at the expression on her face, he very much regretted it. He was behaving like a fool. This was the last thing he needed—reawakening feelings that should have died years ago. And yet. . . . He raised his eyes to hers and felt an almost uncontrollable urge to reach out and touch her face, to draw her close, to see the anger melt into something quite different . . .

Instead, he made a quick gesture of apology.

"As a matter of fact," he said, "it gives me no pleasure at all. And for what it's worth, I'm sorry."

He watched the color recede from her face. The sincerity in his voice hadn't been lost on her, and she was no doubt as keen as he was to depersonalize the conversation and get back to business.

"Apology accepted," she said at last, her voice still a little breathless. "Water under the bridge. Now, perhaps we could just finish off in a positive way?"

"Fire away." He watched her expression as she ploughed on determinedly. Although her eyes met his coolly enough, the quick flick of her hand as she tucked a stray tendril of silky hair behind her ear was a dead giveaway. She was nervous, desperately keen to keep things on a formal basis in which there were clearly defined parameters—where she was doing her job and he was, however reluctant, a mere participant. She was careful to concentrate on his career with special emphasis on his latest films, drawing him out to speak frankly about his working relationships with other stars, about the nuts and bolts of filmmaking. For a while, he felt himself actually beginning to relax—even enjoy himself.

"I'd like, finally," she said, "to ask you about your future plans. If you really are disillusioned with Hollywood and you don't want to return to the theater—then what?"

"I have one or two ideas. But none that I want to share with anyone at the moment."

"Fine. Would you mind, then, if I asked you one or two questions about your life here, in Florida?"

"I thought I'd made it clear. No personal questions."

"I'd just like to know what made you choose to live here in virtual isolation."

He smiled. "Nice try. But forget it, Allegra. I won't budge on that particular subject."

She eyed him thoughtfully, weighing her chances of getting away with one more personal question. "Couldn't I just mention that you have Jack staying with you?"

Max's mouth tightened. She was persistent! No different from the rest of her kind. Determined to ferret out every tiny detail when it was clear he liked to keep his personal life out of the glare of publicity.

"Why can't you accept the fact that I've no intention of providing details about my private life?"

"But why hide the fact that you have a nephew?" She was pushing the boat out farther and farther and she knew it.

Max clenched his jaw. Had they been talking as friends, he might well have confided in her. But at the end of the day, she was a journalist, and the story might just be too good to suppress.

"I have my reasons."

"Such as?"

"You're treading on dangerous ground, Allegra."

"That's what I'm paid to do." She stared at him defiantly. "If I'm to get anything out of this interview, I might as well go for broke—or pack it in and go home."

"That's your choice. I've said all I intend to say on the subject." He shot her a look that might have destroyed the fainthearted.

"Fine! It's just that it would be nice to show you're human, not just some spoiled superstar with a handsome face and a bad attitude."

Their eyes met and locked, and then Max threw back his head and gave a sudden shout of laughter. "You don't pull your punches, do you? Maybe that's why I find you so refreshing by comparison."

"By comparison with?"

"With the kind of women I normally have lunch with."

Her eyes were contemptuous. "Oh, please," she said, "spare me the details. I think they're quite well documented, don't you?"

"Don't tell me your readers wouldn't be interested!" His mouth twitched. It was surprisingly easy to wind her up. He was freewheeling, teasing her again, leading her away from the subject she was most interested in.

"I think I've already explained that I don't work for the gutter press," she said coldly. "And frankly, the way this so-called interview has worked out, I may soon not be working at all. A shame, because until I was given this assignment, I actually enjoyed my job."

The sweet seriousness of her expression captivated him. He wished he was not so deeply aware of her—of the way she moved, of the curve of her mouth, of the subtle perfume she was wearing.

He forced himself to concentrate. "If you insist on focusing on subjects you know are off limits, you have only yourself to blame."

"And if you could just bring yourself to answer a few simple questions instead of continually trying to side-track, the whole thing would be over and done with in half an hour. And then you could get rid of me."

"And what makes you think I want to be rid of you?" Her directness was disarming, but he could deal with that. He was too good an actor not to be able to keep his feelings from showing in his expression. What he couldn't handle was the way that bright, intense gaze triggered something deep inside him, kindling a sudden rush of longing. He leaned across the table and imprisoned both her hands in his. "Listen," he said, "you can have no idea how I felt when I saw you standing there yesterday. I can't help wanting to know what's been happening in your life over the last seven years."

Shocked by the sudden sincerity in his voice, Allegra caught her breath. As she met his glance, her senses stirred with memories so sweet and painful that she wanted to cry out. She had once drowned in those eyes, would have given anything to have spent her entire life with this man.

"Please!" Common sense reasserted itself, but although she managed to free her left hand, he tightened his grip on the other. Slowly, his eyes never leaving her face, he lifted it to his lips.

"For heaven's sake!" Trembling, she snatched her hand away and forced a mocking smile. "What exactly are you trying to do? Convince yourself you haven't lost your touch?"

Max shook his head, looking dazed. "I'm not sure quite what I'm doing. I'm sorry, I seem to have gone a little crazy."

"Oh, please!" She turned her head away, determined not to let him see how deeply he had affected her. "If this is the price I have to pay for this interview, forget it. My job doesn't mean that much to me."

"I'm impressed!" He was quick to recover. "But why

so coy, fair maiden? You're not seventeen anymore. And I'm only human."

"And no doubt you fully expect me to throw myself into your arms?" She threw him a scornful glance.

"You can't blame me, surely, for thinking along those lines? Admit it, the chemistry still works."

"That's history, Max! Perhaps you've forgotten that the last time I saw you, there was another of your victims waiting in the wings. And you were desperate to get rid of me."

Of course he hadn't forgotten! How could he ever forget the sight of her standing there on the doorstep, her eyes pleading with him? The stricken look on her face as she turned away? The brutality of his parting words as she'd hurried off into the night?

"I'm terminating this interview," she told him. "Find someone else to give you a write-up, because suddenly, I've gone right off the idea."

"That's a shame." This time there was no trace of mockery. "Please," he said quietly, "pretend the last few minutes never happened. Let's call a truce. Before I foolishly broke the rules, I was beginning to enjoy this interview."

Allegra's mouth set stubbornly. "Actually, I think we should leave it."

He should let her go, he thought, after they'd waved the waiter with the dessert trolley away and sat in silence, not looking at each other. But somehow, he couldn't rid himself of the thought that if she walked away now, he would have lost something that mattered a great deal.

He raised his head and looked at her across the table

after the waiter had poured their coffee. "I wouldn't have had you down as a quitter."

Allegra threw him a scornful glance. "You can't get blood out of a stone."

He held up his hands in mock surrender. "Okay! I admit, I haven't made it easy for you. But I can do better. Just give me another shot."

She hesitated, torn between her commitment to her job and the need to escape. She didn't trust him an inch, but his expression at the moment was candid enough.

"I'm not sure where this is taking us."

"Why not wait and see?"

As she floundered, Max's cell phone rang. She watched his expression change as he answered it.

"How bad is it?" His voice was taut with anxiety. "Are you sure? Okay. I'm on my way right now."

He shoved the phone back into his pocket and got to his feet. "Jack's fallen out of a tree and hurt himself."

"Oh, no!" Allegra, gazed up at him, concerned.

"Carlos doesn't think it's too bad, but I need to be there."

"Of course."

He hesitated for a second, gazing at her as if he was trying to make up his mind. Then he touched her briefly on the shoulder before turning away. "I'll call you later."

Chapter Five

"**Y**ou have got to be kidding!" Ed was outraged when Max rang to tell him that he hadn't finished the interview. "For Pete's sake, Max, I turn my back for an hour and you go and blow the thing sky high!"

"Slow down! I had to leave it anyway. Jack took a tumble off a tree and sprained his wrist. The little guy was pretty shaken up."

"That kid's more trouble than you can shake a stick at!"

"Nothing I can't handle," Max snapped. "He's my nephew, remember? A lot more important to me than some unnecessary hype. But don't worry, I've taken care of it. I'll finish the interview. Here. Tomorrow."

"At your place?" Ed was incredulous. "Are you crazy? You're letting a journalist into your house? She must be something!"

"Not just any journalist. Allegra and I actually go

way back. We met years ago when I was working in London. And yes, she is, as you say, quite something."

Max was recalling the way he had felt when he had taken her hand and felt it tremble under his lips. He'd wanted to reach for her; to hold her in his arms; to say crazy, extravagant things to her . . .

"And?" Ed demanded.

"And nothing!" Max collected himself with an effort. "Tomorrow," he said with far more conviction than he felt, "we finish the interview. End of story."

Was it? he asked himself as he replaced the receiver. What exactly did he think he was playing at? Did he really need any further complications in his life? Maybe he should have let Allegra go—before it was too late. He was playing a dangerous game, and he knew it. But suddenly, at the thought of seeing her again, he didn't care.

"Buenos dias, señorita!"

Carlos was waiting on the quayside when Allegra arrived at the marina the following morning.

"Good morning." Allegra smiled at him as he helped her into the motorboat.

She stood beside him as he started the engine and began to maneuver his way through the maze of floating jetties.

"Señor Max, he has a good mood this morning!" He grinned. "He looks forward to see you, yes?"

Allegra sighed. How many other females had Carlos ferried across to the island for the pleasure of Max's company?

When she'd heard his voice over the phone last night, her heartbeat had accelerated alarmingly. Deep down she hadn't really expected him to call. The interview had gone so badly that she hadn't anticipated a repeat performance. Besides, she had to admit that whatever image Max projected to the public, he certainly had his priorities right. His little nephew came first.

"Just a few cuts and bruises and a sprained wrist," he'd said when she asked about Jack. "He'll be fine. But Maria was right to call. The little guy was kind of shaken up."

The genuine relief and warmth in his voice had gotten to her. "Are you free tomorrow, to finish the interview? How about if you came over here to the island? Carlos could pick you up at the marina?"

She didn't even hesitate. Suddenly, she felt as high as a kite—as excited and nervous as a teenager about to go on her first date. *Careful,* she told herself. She couldn't allow herself to get all girlish and starry-eyed about Max all over again; having one's heart broken at seventeen was painful. Seven years on, it might just be terminal!

"Have you worked for Mr. Tempest for long?" she asked Carlos as they sped across the sun-dappled water.

"More than three years. He is a good boss. Very kind," Carlos said. "My wife and me—we are lucky."

"Really?"

He nodded. "Last year, my brother—he was very sick. Mr. Max, he helped the family. Took care of the bills and paid the rent until things came better. And now Ramón is okay, he has found him a job working for a big star in Miami. Soon he is moving his family there."

Allegra smiled. Max had a good heart. It was what he did to other people's that caused the problems!

Trailing her hand in the silky water, she watched Shell Island getting closer. Already she was beginning to steel herself to look calmly into that dark, saturnine face. And by the time Carlos was nudging the boat alongside the jetty, she was wishing herself a million miles away.

As she sat waiting on the terrace, Allegra found herself tapping her foot nervously. Furtively she sneaked a glance in her compact mirror, relieved to discover that her face and expression were quite normal. For heaven's sake! After all her careful preparation, she was losing her grip. She should have been e-mailing her article to Helena today. Instead, here she was, up to her neck in trouble, reliving her adolescence and terrified at the thought that after all this time she was still as vulnerable and every bit as susceptible as ever. Max was right about the chemistry between them. It was still there, powerful, persuasive, unchanged. But there was simply no way she could allow herself to show weakness. Yesterday, he had taken her by surprise. But from now on, she'd be on her guard. Forewarned was forearmed.

The sudden appearance of Jack sporting a bruised cheek and a heavily bandaged right arm jolted Allegra out of her stream of thought.

"Wow!" She looked impressed. "That looks serious!"

Jack nodded proudly. "I was trying to climb to the top of a pine tree, and a branch broke off. I fell and busted my arm. It hurt. A lot. And," he added significantly, "there was blood."

"Really?"

Jack displayed the impressive dressing happily. "I could take this off and show it to you if you want."

"That's okay." Allegra shook her head. "You'd better keep the dressing on. That way, it will heal up more quickly. I suppose you won't be able to go swimming for a while."

"It's just a sprain." Max was striding across the terrace toward them. He put his arm around his nephew and gave his baseball cap a tweak. "It'll soon heal up, won't it, champ?"

Jack frowned, and his bottom lip protruded almost aggressively. He looked as if he was about to say something, but then, clearly annoyed, he turned and marched off across the terrace.

"What did I say?" Max looked after him in amazement.

Allegra grinned. "Don't you remember how important a bandage made you feel when you were Jack's age? It isn't a good idea to trivialize his injury like that."

Max sighed, shaking his head. "I guess I have a lot to learn! Anyway, how come you're such an authority?"

"I have a raft of nephews and nieces—some around Jack's age—and I'm the best babysitter in town."

Max looked at her speculatively. "I don't doubt that." He sighed. "Jack can be a handful."

"Like all small boys."

"Maybe. But he sure gave me a scare yesterday. How exactly am I supposed to keep track of his every movement?"

Allegra noted with a certain wry amusement the look

of bewilderment in his eyes. She laughed. "With difficulty, I imagine. But you'll learn."

"Let's hope so. Anyway, shall we begin again? Good morning." The eyes swept her with undisguised appreciation. Allegra was dressed casually in cropped jeans and a plain white T-shirt, which revealed a couple of inches of toned midriff and emphasized her tiny waist.

She returned his gaze steadily. "It's good of you to invite me here. My editor will be delighted."

Max grinned. "And grateful, I hope. I suppose she'll realize how privileged you are? I don't exactly make a habit of inviting members of your profession into my home."

"I think I got that."

"Can I offer you coffee, or shall we just get on with it?"

"I'm happy to begin right away." She reached into her bag and took out her cassette recorder.

Max shook his head, grinning. "You won't need that today." He took her arm, drawing her to her feet. "Follow me." The smile creased the tanned skin around his eyes, lifted a corner of his mouth, and forced her to concentrate on her breathing.

"Where are we going?" Allegra felt the familiar panic rising at the touch of his fingers on her skin.

"Relax!" He jerked his head in the direction of the steps leading down to the sea. "I'm about to introduce you to my one true love. Can't get more personal than that, can I?"

Allegra caught her breath. The sudden sharp stab of pain felt shockingly like pure unadulterated jealousy. She hadn't bargained for this! So this is that what he had meant by becoming more personal? If so, she wasn't at all sure she wanted to know.

But if Max was really serious about this woman, why was he suddenly being so open? It didn't make sense, she thought, as she stumbled down the uneven steps in his wake. This has to be some kind of windup.

By the time she had reached the last step, he was pulling open the heavy door of a weathered wooden building—the last place Allegra would have imagined meeting one of Max's glamorous girlfriends.

"Hurry," he said over his shoulder, "come and meet Miranda, the only lady in my life."

Allegra looked in through the open door. For a second or two, her mind went blank and then she caught her breath in amazed admiration. There, rocking gently in the water, lay the sloop, *Miranda* picked out in white at the stern. She was, as Max had said, a lady—every elegant inch of her.

"Well? What do you think? She handles," Max said with pride, "like a dream."

Allegra stared as if mesmerized at Miranda's gleaming brass and burnished teak. The sleek craft really was a beauty, the hull sea green with a narrow white line just above the watermark.

"I thought . . ." she stammered, "I imagined. . . ." Her voice trailed off in confusion.

Max laughed. "I can guess what you thought. But believe it or not, *Miranda* really is the only lady in my life—at the moment."

"Really?" She hadn't meant to sound quite so cynical.

"If you want to believe everything that's printed

about me, that's your problem." He shrugged. "The most important thing in my life at the moment is taking care of my nephew." He went on. "I promised my sister I'd look out for him. And that's what I plan on doing."

Allegra knew by the closed expression on his face that it would be sheer folly to attempt to push for more information, although a dozen questions rushed through her mind. But Max was staring at *Miranda,* his face an unreadable mask.

"I hope you're a good sailor," he said. "If we're going to take her out, we'd better get on with it."

"Out? You mean a sailing trip?" Allegra gave a nervous start.

"Why not? Isn't this the personal touch you wanted for your readers?" he asked impatiently.

Allegra stared at him in horrified disbelief. The closest she'd ever come to sailing was a brief and disastrous holiday on the River Fal in Cornwall. The mysteries of tying knots and hooking up buoys had completely defeated her—she didn't know a sheet from a shroud—and the memory of her struggles with that confusing tangle of ropes filled her with alarm.

But Max was already vaulting lightly over the rail and offering her a hand. And as she scrambled into the swaying boat, she inwardly cursed herself for letting matters get this far. She really had intended to keep things simple. And now here she was, embarking on a sailing trip alone with the very man she wanted to keep at arm's length.

"Scared?" Max, still holding her right hand in a

warm, firm clasp, was looking down into her tense face with every sign of amused satisfaction.

"Not in the least," she retorted, steadying herself as she felt the boat tilt under her feet.

She watched, fascinated, as he began to get the boat under way, admiring the deft movements of his square brown hands on the ropes, the look of total absorption on the dark, intent face. As he pushed open the heavy sea doors and poled *Miranda* out into the open sea, Allegra realized that this was Max's element. He was as much at home on the water as he was on stage.

When the engine roared to life, *Miranda* came alive, slipping out into the sunlit bay. And Allegra, a silent spectator, understood that Max was allowing her to share an experience not normally accorded to anyone except, perhaps, his most intimate friends.

She sat in the bows, listening to the creak of timber, responding to the swaying movement of the graceful craft as Max turned her head to the wind and put up the mainsail.

"Want to take a turn?" Max yelled from the stern, gesturing at the tiller, and she shook her head. It was easy to understand why she had once fallen so deeply in love with him. He was so uncompromisingly male—so utterly in control of every situation. She would have to be careful, she thought. He knew only too well how to use his power over women—and women far more sophisticated than herself!

Half an hour later, with the wind beginning to drop, Max took in the mainsail and anchored off Coral, a tiny island a few miles due south. Allegra, staring across the implausible blues and greens of the calm expanse of water, was beginning to feel an increasing sense of unreality. It was hard to believe that she was actually here, sharing this exotic paradise with Max, and she jumped nervously as he suddenly came up behind her.

"What do you think?" he asked. "Personal enough for you?"

"Quite personal enough, thanks." She kept her voice and manner casual. "How fast will she go?"

"Eight knots under sail. It's a pity the wind's dropping. But it often happens this time of the day. The air gets very still, and then there's usually a thunderstorm."

Allegra glanced up doubtfully at the cloudless blue sky. "Then isn't it time we were getting back?"

"We have plenty of time. How about a swim?"

"A swim?" Allegra stared at him, alarmed. "What do you suggest I wear?"

He grinned, clearly amused by the fearful expression in her eyes. "You object to skinny-dipping?"

"Don't be absurd." Allegra reddened.

"I'm kidding!" He was laughing openly at her outraged expression. "You'll find a suit below in one of the lockers. In fact, there are several. There's bound to be one that fits."

Allegra hesitated. All this, she thought, just for a couple thousand words! Still, a swim did sound inviting.

Once below, she found herself utterly captivated by the layout and the streamlined delights of the compact little galley with its immaculate built-in equipment: fridge, oven, ceramic range—even a dishwasher and tiny microwave. There were windows on either side of the cabin and, beneath them, cushioned berths. Between them was a table made of highly polished teak, and beyond them a doorway leading to another tiny cabin and an immaculate bathroom with gleaming white tiles. The whole place was a masterpiece of design, and there appeared to be more storage than Allegra had in her own London apartment.

After rummaging in a locker in the forward berth, Allegra discovered a collection of swimsuits and swimming trunks. Obviously Max often sailed with friends aboard, and judging by some of the bikinis, the females were obviously of the uninhibited variety. She finally came up with a plain black one-piece, that looked about her size and closeted herself in the tiny berth while she stripped off.

After she had struggled into the suit, she stared critically at her modestly clad limbs in the long mirror behind the door. Thank heaven she had shed the few extra pounds she had put on during the winter. Still, did it really matter? Max, naturally, would be used to entertaining far more seductive women on his boat—if the procession of suntanned beauties he was constantly being photographed with was anything to go by.

Max was mesmerized by the sight of the woman who had disturbed his sleep and troubled his dreams for the past couple of nights. The reality, as she stood there in the simple black suit, which revealed nothing more than the slim perfection of her figure, was far more appealing. Allegra fired something buried deep inside him—something far more potent than the natural male response to a beautiful woman.

He turned and pulled off his T-shirt, sliding the blue jeans down over his narrow hips to reveal dark blue swimming trunks.

"Ready?" he asked casually, over his shoulder.

"Yes."

She walked to the edge of the swimming platform and then, without further ado, made a perfectly executed dive into the calm blue water, surfacing twenty feet away, and struck out strongly for the shore.

She had covered fifty yards before Max caught up, and she turned, treading water, as his head bobbed up beside her.

"What was that all about?" He was gasping a little from the exertion he had expended in chasing her. "Don't you know you should never dive into cold water when your body is overheated?"

Allegra gave him a scornful grin. "It doesn't seem to have done me much harm."

"But it might have." He swam closer, tossing a strand of wet black hair out of his eyes. "The shock of cold water on hot skin can stop your heart."

"But it didn't." Her mouth was infinitely enticing, curved—an invitation to kiss her to distraction. He saw her eyes widen as she read his expression, but he was too late to avoid the spray of water she flicked at him. He reached out impulsively to grab her but she was gone, slipping, quicksilver, from his arms and continuing toward shore. This time, it was easier to overtake her with his long, powerful strokes, leaving her to follow in his wake. Reaching the shallows, he stood up, the water streaming silver from his bronzed torso, and waded ashore. He made his way up the beach without a backward look and flung himself facedown in the shade of the palms.

When she joined him, they lay there in silence for a while, the green shadows of the trees flickering over their bodies.

Max, having gotten his breathing under control, raised his head and looked at her obliquely.

"You're quite a strong swimmer," he said.

Allegra shrugged. "I used to do quite a bit of competition swimming when I was younger."

"Really?" He raised his eyebrows in surprise. "I never saw you as an athletic type. You looked quite uncomfortable on the boat."

"I never learned to sail. I'm a country girl, remember? I actually prefer horses."

"I have a place in Wyoming you'd enjoy." He could see her astride a horse, he thought, with the wind in her hair. "I'm left alone when I go there. Too far off the beaten track for the newshounds, I guess."

Then, catching the faintly mocking expression on her face, "You wouldn't know what it's like to be hunted down and spied on continually. To have elaborate stories concocted about you. To be constantly misquoted in newspapers and misrepresented all over the world."

"But you must have known you'd be in for that sort of thing when you decided to become part of the movie industry."

"I was green as grass in those days. But now I know

that as long as I'm tied to a contract, I'm fair game. I have to endure the publicity—good and bad. But I don't have to like it, and I'll use any means in my power to avoid it."

"Let's see." Her eyes sparkled with mischief. "Like walking off set in the middle of a TV talk show? Like grabbing someone's camera and aiming it at his head?"

He grinned. "I missed. Anyway, it was an isolated incident and I was provoked. I don't normally go in for violence. These days, I try to avoid the media—which is one of the reasons why I left L.A. and bought a house on an island. I had an apartment in New York, but I don't spend much time there, so I sold it a few months ago."

"And Jack," Allegra said, "didn't he say he lived in New York?"

Was she merely doing her job or deliberately hassling him? Having found his Achilles' heel, was she quietly letting him know that she could, if she wished, cause him a great deal of trouble?

"Let's not go there again," he said sharply. "I've bent over backward to give you an angle. The least you can do is keep to the rules."

"I'd do that if they made any sense."

"They make perfect sense and you know it. I've had too many bad experiences with people in your profession to want to bare my soul to your public, believe me!"

"I was just asking about your nephew, Max, not your immortal soul!"

He glared at her. "If you push me too hard, you might end up with nothing!"

"Don't lose your temper," Allegra said calmly. "I'm

just trying to do my job. Anyway, I can't help being interested. Jack's a sweetheart and I happen to like kids."

"In that case, why haven't you taken the necessary steps to acquire some of your own?" Max laughed triumphantly at her outraged expression. "You see? It's not pleasant, is it? Being asked personal questions?"

"But I'm not the one being interviewed!"

Max grinned. "Sorry. Just as a matter of interest," he mocked.

"I take your point," she said coldly. "All right—I have nothing to hide—there was someone I thought I might marry. But I—we split up a few months ago."

"Painful?" Why did he feel as if he'd been kicked hard in the stomach? Had he actually imagined there had been no one in her life for the last seven years?

"It hurt, yes. We'd been together quite a while."

"So are you going to tell me to mind my own business if I asked you why it ended?"

Allegra shook her head, her blue eyes candid. "Not at all. It's not a secret. There were just some pretty fundamental differences in what we wanted out of life."

"Such as?" he prompted.

"I wanted children. Simon didn't. As simple as that."

He watched the faint color in her cheeks with a sudden pang. Seven years on, he'd somehow assumed that she'd grown harder, more ambitious, with the sharp edges often seen in career women of her type.

Instead, he realized, the essential sweetness of her nature had never changed. Behind the sophisticated veneer, she was as natural and unaffected as ever.

"So were you in love with this guy?" he asked, his

voice carefully casual. He must, he thought, have been a jerk.

"For a while I thought I was. But we couldn't work it out. I love kids, and I couldn't contemplate marriage without them."

Suddenly, Max had a mental picture of Allegra running through grass in bright sunshine, surrounded by laughing kids.

He picked up a handful of tiny, gleaming shells and let them run slowly through the long fingers. "I never realized how important kids were until Jack came along. He means a lot to me. Taking care of him, as you've probably realized, doesn't come easy, but I'm working on it." He paused, glanced at her quickly, and then as if suddenly casting caution to the winds, "His mother died a year ago. She was my kid sister."

Allegra stared at Max in horror. "That's dreadful! I'm so sorry."

"It was tough on us both—but worse for the little guy, naturally. I was in New Zealand, filming, when it happened. I only just managed to make it home for the funeral."

He answered the unspoken question in her eyes. "My sister was a single parent. Right now Jack is being raised in a foster home. I had to move heaven and earth to get him out of there for a few weeks." Max frowned. What exactly did he think he was doing? If he carried on like this, she'd soon have the story of his life on a plate. The conversation was getting far too intimate.

He sat up. "I hope you understand that all that was

strictly off the record? I want to give Jack a good time. It's impossible to make up for all that he's been through— but at least I can show him I care." He dusted the sand from his fingers. "Okay. I've said all I want to say on the subject. End of interview. How hard would it be to pretend from now on that we were just two people enjoying each other's company?"

Allegra's heart ached for poor little Jack. No wonder Max wanted to protect him. Clearly, he wanted to do his best for his nephew. But would this vacation together be just a one-off? Surely Max's lifestyle would make it almost impossible to keep in close contact with the little boy. Was that why he was thinking of ending his career?

She glanced up and saw the faintly cynical expression on his face. "Now what?"

Allegra smiled, not daring to share her thoughts. "Just one more thing." She paused. "All those wild parties and beautiful girls I've read about?"

"All part of the myth dreamed up to create the authentic Hollywood image. I loathe parties and try to avoid them. As for the beautiful girls—frankly, I've always preferred women my own age.

Allegra blushed to the roots of her hair, and Max could have bitten out his tongue as soon as the words were out.

"Wait. I didn't mean . . . I wasn't referring to . . ."

He stopped, floundering, and there was silence as she fought an acute desire to kick sand in his face. That last comment of his might have been entirely ingenuous. Maybe he hadn't planned to offend her. Anyway, it was ridiculous to let it bother her after all this time!

"Isn't it about time we got back to the boat?" She was already on her feet. "Before the weather turns ugly?"

"You're right." He stood up, his tall figure blocking out the sun. He grinned. "I don't believe I could rely on you to crew for me in a thunderstorm!"

Max was tinkering with the engine when she joined him on board.

"When you've changed, you'll find some cold drinks in the fridge," he said. "Help yourself."

"Thanks." Allegra hesitated. "What about the thunderstorm?"

"We've an hour or so, at least."

She hovered for a moment or two, watching him at his task as he knelt on deck. Her eyes traced the line of the muscular shoulders, ran down the length of the bronzed back to the pale line just above the swim trunks where his suntan ended. Max, sensing her eyes on him, threw her a quick glance over his shoulder. Quickly, she turned in sudden confusion and disappeared rapidly below.

She went into the forward berth and stripped off her wet suit. So what? she asked herself, rubbing herself vigorously with a rough towel. Just because she was attracted to a good-looking man didn't mean a thing. She was human, wasn't she? How many red-blooded women could ignore the physical appeal of a man as attractive as Max Tempest? Her cheeks flamed as she remembered the way he had tried to take hold of her in the water. For a moment, she'd almost. . . . Stop! She pressed her hands against her hot face. If Max was deliberately reawakening feelings that had died long ago, then it was up to her to stamp them out. All she had to do was finish writing the article and get it to Helena. Then she could turn her back on the wretched man for good.

Allegra tied back her damp hair and gave herself a determined little nod in the mirror. Then she went into the galley to explore the interior of the fridge. An unopened jar of beluga caviar dominated the top shelf, and a six-pack of cola rubbed shoulders, rather incongruously, with a bottle of Dom Perignon. On the bottom shelf was a large a tin of anchovies, a box of eggs, an overripe avocado, and some bottled water. It was just as well, she thought wryly, that she wasn't in the least hungry. The short stack of pancakes she'd devoured for breakfast had seen to that! In England pancakes meant something quite different, and her father had always insisted on making them U.S. style, with plenty of maple syrup!

She was about to reach for the water when Max's legs, now clad in jeans, appeared on the ladder.

"Sorry the cupboard's so bare," he said with a rueful grin. "I keep meaning to stock up, but I'm not much of a cook, as you can see. If you're starving, I could probably rustle up a half-decent omelet. But then any fool can do that."

"Not true. They say that the ability to make a really good omelet is the sign of true culinary greatness. But don't worry, I'm not hungry, so you're off the hook."

"Then I think it must be the champagne, don't you? After all, this is, in a sense, a celebration."

"Is it?" Allegra looked blank.

"Our reunion after seven years." He held up the bottle. "You approve, I hope?"

Allegra shrugged. "I know next to nothing about champagne."

The conversation was making her feel faintly uncomfortable. The atmosphere was beginning to feel much too cozy, and as he took out the champagne, she hoped that this sudden relaxation of formality between them was not a prelude to something more intimate.

She jumped when he suddenly moved behind her and she felt his hands on her waist. He was merely attempting to squeeze past her to get to the drawer that housed the bottle opener, but the brief contact threw her.

If Max noticed, he made no comment, uncorked the bottle, and poured the champagne. He raised his glass. "What shall we drink to? Old acquaintance?"

Still struggling to regain composure, she clinked her glass against his and repeated the phrase like an automaton. "Old acquaintance."

They sat down opposite each other on the cushioned berths at either side of the drop leaf table, and Allegra quickly steered the conversation to neutral ground: a recent West End play about to move to New York. The latest Ian McEwan novel. A trip she'd taken to Venice.

"A top-up?" Max asked her, gesturing at her unfinished drink.

She smiled, shaking her head. "I'm afraid it's wasted on me."

He nodded. "I'm not a connoisseur either." He got to his feet, steadying himself as the boat suddenly tilted.

"It's time we were making for home. I think the storm's about to hit."

When Allegra went on deck ten minutes later, she was alarmed at the sudden change in the weather. The sea was the color of pewter, the sky like brass, and the atmosphere distinctly menacing.

"We'll run for cover," Max said as he started the engine. "We should just make it to my place, but there won't be time to get you back to Cedar Bay before the storm breaks."

He was right. They had scarcely reached the boathouse before the first enormous drops of rain began to fall, and Allegra gave a nervous jump at the deep rumble of thunder.

Carlos was waiting, ready to help secure the sea doors.

Max glanced upward at the inky sky. "We'd better get indoors. It's going to cut loose any minute."

Even as he spoke, the rain began in earnest, accompanied by a low rumble of thunder and then the first white flash of lightning. Max reached for her hand, and then, as they fled up the stone steps, came the deluge—a sudden drenching downpour, the drops of rain huge and heavy and unrelenting.

Inside the house, they stood gasping—hair plastered to their heads, sodden clothes clinging to their bodies. Max grinned at the expression of horrified amazement on Allegra's face, and suddenly they were both helpless, clutching each other for support, racked by gales of uncontrollable laughter.

As she clung to him, the laughter died on her lips and she saw what was coming. It was too late to take evasive action, even if she'd wanted to. Max lifted a hand, twisting his fingers in her hair, holding her captive. This time there was no trace of mockery in his eyes as he bent his head to kiss her, and she responded instinctively to the warm pressure of his mouth. For a few seconds she was entirely his, and she shook as she felt his hand brush her cheek in a caress that made her head spin.

And then the outer door flung open and Carlos burst in.

"Pardon!" His face was a comical mixture of dismay and delight as they sprang apart. There was a brief, awkward silence, and then Max looked at him impassively. "Show Miss Howard upstairs to the guest room, would you, please? She'll need to get out of her wet clothes."

Carlos nodded, trying to hide his amusement. "Of course."

"You'll find a robe behind the door," Max said. "And Carlos will get your clothes dried."

"Thanks." With averted eyes, she brushed past Max and headed in the direction of the cloakroom.

The bedraggled creature in the full-length mirror, Allegra saw ruefully, was hardly an encouraging sight. She took a deep, calming breath. Carlos had made his entry in the nick of time! She passed a shaky hand over her lips, still tingling from Max's kiss. What was she thinking? Did he merely have to take her in his arms to make her act like a besotted schoolgirl all over again?

Of course not! It would take more than a few kisses to make that happen! They had spent far too much time alone together today, with too many echoes of the past. She was just a little confused, that was all.

She grabbed a towel to dry her hair, brushing it back from her face, and let the damp wavy tresses cascade over her shoulders. Then, clad in the outsize bathrobe, she marched boldly out into the hall in search of Carlos, who took her wet clothes to be dried with a distinctly knowing grin.

Chapter Six

"The storm's passing." Max turned from the window as she entered the room.

The view, Allegra noted, was not encouraging. The sea was a deep green with angry white-topped waves—a far cry from the calm blue water of an hour ago.

"In ten minutes the sun will be out," Max said, "and there won't be a cloud in the sky. Florida is a place of extremes."

"Living here wouldn't suit me, then," Allegra said, joining him on the sofa. "I like moderation, I'm afraid."

"That must be the English half of you. The reserved, rather proper part that surfaces now and again."

She smiled. "And the American half?"

"That's the part I knew in London. Much more relaxed." His eyes teased her. "Perhaps even a little wild."

"Not anymore." Allegra kept her face carefully expressionless. It was difficult to remain cool and detached when he was sitting so close to her. "People change. They grow up—learn to behave in a more sensible, rational way."

"Kind of sad, isn't it?"

"Not really. Personally, I'd hate to be that age again. All that angst and uncertainty! Yuck!"

He gestured for her to sit with him on the sofa, and she suddenly realized how hungry she was when Carlos arrived with a knowing smile and a tray of sandwiches and coffee.

"Thank you." Allegra couldn't quite meet those mischievous black eyes!

Max held out his cup for Allegra to pour, and there was something about the casual intimacy of the gesture that made her feel warm inside.

"What were we saying?" he asked. "Oh, yes. Growing up. Well, I don't believe anyone really changes their character. Given the right sort of stimulus, I guess they always revert to type."

What was this leading to? "Do they?" Allegra met the sardonic gray eyes warily.

He laughed softly. "You know I'm right. Underneath that cool, professional mask is a seventeen-year-old Allegra just waiting to be invited to emerge in all her glory."

Max suddenly leaned toward her and gently brushed back a damp tendril of hair from her hot face.

Allegra grabbed the coffee pot although her cup was still half full—anything to keep him at arm's length! Was this the prelude to something she knew she had to avoid?

"There was nothing glorious about me when I was seventeen!" she snapped. "In fact, I was rather a country

mouse! Being raised in the depths of the English coun-
tryside didn't exactly prepare me for survival in the big
city."

"No more than life on a farm in Nebraska prepared
me for the theater. There were times, at the beginning,
when I just wanted to turn and run back home." Max
laughed softly. "In fact, there are still moments when I
would like to do exactly that."

"You mean that?" Allegra was struck by the look of
nostalgia on his face.

"I guess so. Not that it would be possible. The farm
was sold when my father died some years ago." He
smiled rather diffidently. "Occasionally I have fantasies
about buying it back and spending the rest of my life
raising cattle. Crazy, isn't it?"

Allegra smiled at the sudden incongruous image of
Max herding cows in a pasture. "But I know what you
mean. I miss the country too," she said. "Though I enjoy the experience of working in London. It was hard at
first, of course. And I made some stupid mistakes."

Max raised his eyebrow. "I take it I was one of them?"

Allegra swallowed hard. In that one short sentence,
the atmosphere between them had changed. He had
thrown down the gauntlet, and she knew she would be
unable to resist picking it up.

"Yes," she said, looking him straight in the eye. "I'm
afraid you were."

"Really?" He gave her a sardonic glance. "Was it my
fault that you decided to lie about your age and throw
yourself at the first reasonably presentable man to show
interest?"

Oh, Lord. She'd touched a nerve this time! And he was right. Much as she hated to admit it, she'd done exactly what he'd accused her of. And his behavior, in fairness, had been impeccable. But had he really no idea how much he'd hurt her? How painful she had found the rejection? How humiliated she had felt when he had so casually discarded her? She'd been in love for the first time, and he must have known it. And he'd moved on so quickly to his next victim. And how long had she lasted? Allegra wondered.

She looked at him coldly. "The fault was mine. I'm well aware of that."

"And if you remember," he added, "I did have the decency to let you off the hook."

She flinched. Why were they doing this yet again? Dredging up the past—stirring up things best left unsaid?

"This conversation is pointless." Her voice was dismissive. "I think we've both said all we need to say on the subject, don't you?"

He shrugged. "I wasn't the one who brought it up."

"I know. Perhaps I just wanted you to understand that I learned my lesson all those years ago."

His mouth twitched. "Forgive me if I appear a tad skeptical."

Allegra reddened. "Excuse me?"

"I didn't imagine your reaction to that kiss a little while ago." Max shrugged.

"Really?" She forced herself to meet his cool, compelling glance. "Don't flatter yourself. You caught me off guard, that's all."

She glanced at her watch. "Heavens! Is that the time?"

Why did her voice sound so high and unnatural? "I really ought to get back and file my article."

"I hope you're satisfied with the material you have."

"It'll do."

"And, at the risk of repeating myself, I expect you to stick to the deal. No mention of Jack. Or my family."

"That's a pity."

The gray eyes iced over. "I mean it, Allegra. Once they knew he was here, the papparazi would zoom in like a swarm of bees 'round a honey pot."

Allegra acknowledged, with the briefest nod of her head, that he was right. She knew journalists who would quite callously ignore Max's wishes. He was a tempting target, and if he showed the tiniest chink in his protective armor, they would be in like a flash. There was no way she could bring herself to betray his secret.

"I must be in the wrong job." She sighed. "Helena will probably sack me when the story breaks. Oh, yes, Max!" She saw his quick gesture of denial. "You won't escape for long. You should know how hard it is to conceal anything from the press. But for Jack's sake, I'll do what you ask." She got to her feet. "Now, would you please get hold of Carlos and my clothes? I've got work to do."

Max walked slowly to the end of the jetty, staring across the sea until the boat was out of sight.

Both searching for suitable exit lines, they had said their good-byes with grave formality. Now he felt empty and morose. He, who had craved solitude and space, was suddenly bereft. He frowned, kicked a pebble into the water, heard its soft splash, followed it with another and another. A restless discontent had overtaken him. Suddenly the things that gave him most pleasure—music, books, a glass or two of fine wine—seemed utterly banal. So what exactly did he want? He knew, only too well. He wanted Allegra Howard. And not just as a diversion.

Hadn't she been there always, just out of focus, shadowy, insubstantial, a reminder of what they could have had together if circumstances had been different? But it was too late now. Life rarely handed out second chances. On that thought, he thrust his hands deep into his pockets and began to walk slowly back to the house.

The sight of the small figure hurrying toward him lifted his spirits.

"Hey!" Jack fell in step beside him, his short legs working overtime to keep up.

Max punched his shoulder lightly. "Hey, yourself."

"I was gonna say hi to that lady, but I guess she left. Did she finish the story?"

"You know," Max said, "I guess she did."

Jack glanced up at his uncle's face critically. "Is that why you're ticked?"

Max looked at him, startled. A pretty perceptive remark for a seven-year-old. "What gave you that idea? I was just wondering what we should do today."

"You were?"

Max nodded. "Okay, bud, how about a trip to Clearwater? I guess that new game we ordered for the Nintendo came in."

"Cool!" The small face lit up, and Jack held up his left hand for a high five. Max's heart contracted.

This kid needed him. Come to think of it, it was mutual.

Allegra turned the air conditioner up a couple of notches, kicked off her sandals, and stretched out on her bed.

Burying her hot face in the pillow, she went over the events of the day. How easy would it be to write about Max without her own confused feelings getting in the way? Here she was, lying on her bed like some confused adolescent, incapable at the moment of rational thought.

The memory of that last distressing meeting all those years ago when Allegra was a tongue-tied wreck and Max so remote and utterly controlled suddenly stirred her painfully.

She still went hot when she recalled the day she had plucked up her courage and arrived at Max's flat uninvited and unannounced, like some pitiful stalker blind to the indignity of her situation.

She'd rung the bell several times, staring up in nervous anticipation at the tall Victorian house in the tree-lined London street, remembering how she'd felt the last time Max had taken her there. He had swept a pile of books and scripts off the battered sofa in the shabby, high-ceilinged room and taken her in his arms, held her close, his cheek against her hair. Wrapped in the warmth of his tenderness, she had never felt such complete happiness. How could she ever have imagined that, only weeks later, she would be standing there in the rain, a pitiful, pleading creature praying that Max would welcome her in?

She had begun to turn away, wretched with disappointment, when he'd suddenly opened the door, his eyes registering not just surprise but something far more significant. Even now, Allegra remembered exactly how he had looked—the white shirt, unbuttoned, revealing the muscular chest, blue jeans without a belt, bare brown feet, one lock of glossy black hair hanging over his forehead.

She heard his quick intake of breath.

"Allegra! What are you doing here?" His voice was husky with some kind of emotion she couldn't quite identify.

"Max. . . ." She could feel the blood drumming in her head. "I hadn't seen you for ages," she stammered, all her carefully rehearsed words forgotten. "So I thought . . . I wondered if we could talk . . . if you fancied going out. . . ." Her voice, now little more than a whisper, trailed off miserably as she saw the expression on his face.

"Look, I'm sorry. . . ." He frowned, one hand rubbing the back of his head, and so obviously ill at ease that Allegra found it hard to keep looking at him. She was bitterly regretting the madness that had driven her to this.

"This is a bad time," he muttered, with a quick glance over his shoulder.

Even then, Allegra failed to grasp the significance of

his obvious embarrassment. She took a deep breath. It was now or never. She simply could not go until she had said what she needed to say.

"Max—about the other night. . . ." She forced herself to look directly into his eyes and felt her heart plummet as she saw the shutters come down. One hand reached up to rest against the doorjamb, and he leaned against it, his body language awkward and defensive.

"I think that's best forgotten, don't you?" He smiled, a cold, forced smile. "Look, I'm sorry if you think I'm rude but . . ."

"Of course not!" She felt the color drain from her face. "I shouldn't have come."

It was as she was about to turn away, blind with misery and shame, that she heard the girl's voice.

"Max! Who is it?"

"Nobody!" He looked at Allegra's stricken face and sighed.

"Go home, Allegra," he said fiercely. "And stay out of things you don't understand."

It was only after she'd half walked, half run to the tube station that the tears spilled out over her hot cheeks. Nobody! That's who she was! What a complete idiot she'd made of herself. No doubt at that very moment Max and his impatient girlfriend were laughing together over the pathetic performance she'd just given.

But despite her pain and humiliation, as she sat staring at the floor on the journey home, there was a kind of relief in acknowledging that Julia had been right. It was over. She never wanted to lay eyes on Max Tempest ever again, she told herself, fumbling for a tissue to wipe her tearstained face. The pleasant-faced, middle-aged woman sitting opposite her watched her with undisguised compassion. And when Allegra, suddenly aware of her scrutiny, finally managed to look up, the woman smiled kindly.

"He's not worth it, dear, whoever he is," she'd whispered. "Trust me."

"Your nightcap, señor." Carlos brought Max his usual small Scotch and soda, a taste he'd acquired in London all those years ago.

"Thanks." Max, standing on the terrace, staring moodily into the darkness, was still in evening clothes. "Have you checked on Jack?"

"Sí, señor. He is fast asleep. I have turned out the light."

"By the way, I've been meaning to ask you—how's your brother doing?"

Carlos smiled. "He's doing great. Things are good for him, thanks to you." He paused. "I was going to ask you, señor, if I could take a couple of days to help him move his family to Miami?"

"Sure. Go whenever you want. This week, maybe?"

"A million thanks, señor, for all that you have done. How can we ever repay you? You have been so generous."

"No problem." Max, embarrassed, shook his head. He was fond of both Carlos and his wife, and had been glad to help. "I think that's it for tonight, Carlos. I would turn in if I were you."

Carlos nodded with a thoughtful expression on his face. About to turn away, he hesitated. "The lady—she is very beautiful, señor."

Max glanced at him quickly. "Yes," he said, "she certainly is."

Alone again in the darkness, he grinned ruefully. So the effect of Allegra's reappearance in his life must be pretty obvious! Jack had him all figured out and now Carlos as well. Maybe it was time he stopped behaving like some lovesick teenager. Take tonight, for instance. He had enjoyed the party Ed had insisted that he attend even less than usual. Showbiz gatherings always bored him, and he had found himself mentally comparing every woman in the room with Allegra. He had slipped away from the lavish affair—hosted by a wealthy politician—as soon as was decently possible, and when he'd returned to find Jack still awake and demanding his attention, he'd been sharp with the boy—too sharp—and had immediately regretted it.

Max sighed. There were times when he doubted the wisdom of what he was trying to do. Much as he wanted Jack to be a part of his life, his inexperience with kids showed, and he was sometimes clumsy in handling him. It seemed to come so naturally to some. Take Allegra, for instance. She had struck up an easy camaraderie with Jack within minutes, had established rapport with him quite effortlessly.

At the thought of her, Max closed his eyes, shaking his head as if somehow he could banish all traces of what he was feeling from his mind. He glanced at his watch. Past midnight and yet he had no desire to sleep.

He knew what was bothering him. It was a long time since he had wanted a woman—and he did not mean that in the physical sense. Tonight he felt a longing for something more—the simple pleasure of a woman's presence, the touch of a soft hand in his, the kind of warmth and intimacy which had come only once, very briefly, into his life.

He couldn't let Allegra Howard walk away from him again. Not without some kind of closure. Otherwise, he told himself, he would always wonder what might have been . . .

He put down his drink untasted. What on earth was his problem? He was kidding himself, surely, by imagining that the brief little affair with a seventeen-year-old girl had mattered so much? He remembered so clearly the first time he had set eyes on her. A face in a crowd. A pair of fine eyes. A golden girl in a plain white shirt with pale, shining hair caught back from her face.

Max remembered every detail of the scene backstage at the Globe. He'd looked up just as if he was expecting to find the girl standing there. Their eyes had met and held, and in those few moments he had noticed everything about her: Her flawless skin. Her smile. The sweet curve of her mouth. The slender lines of her body. And he knew that had she been surrounded by the most glittering array of stars of stage and screen, he would only have had eyes for her. Allegra. Even her name was like a piece of music.

"For Pete's sake, get a grip," he muttered. He shrugged out of his dinner jacket and black tie, pulled his shirt over his head, unzipped his pants, and threw the lot over a chair. Then, blotting out the image of Allegra's face from his mind, he went to the edge of the pool and dived in.

Allegra woke with a start at the insistent ringing of the phone on her bedside table. She hadn't meant to fall asleep in the middle of the afternoon, she'd intended to finish the piece on Max, and now she'd wasted almost two hours!

She fumbled for the receiver, struggling to identify the caller's voice.

"Allegra? I've been trying to reach you all day."

"I'm sorry," she muttered, still half asleep. "Who is this?"

"It's Rick. Rick Fielding."

Allegra sat up, suddenly recognizing the soft Irish brogue. "Rick? Good Lord! Where are you calling from?"

She hadn't set eyes on Rick Fielding for months. She'd gotten to know him when she'd landed her first job at *Elegance*. Charming, funny, he was what was usually described as a lovable Irish rogue. She liked him well enough—he was great fun—but he was also totally unreliable, and she wouldn't trust him an inch!

"I'm in Clearwater doing some work for a book on deep sea fishing." Rick was now a successful freelance photographer with the kind of talent that meant he was constantly in demand. "I spoke to Helena a few days ago, and she told me you were out here, so I thought I'd give you a call."

"It's good to hear from you. How's the work going?"

"I finish here tomorrow. Then I'm off to the Keys for a couple of weeks."

"Sounds exciting."

"It is, but before I go, I thought we might be able to get together. I take it you're not exactly rushing back to London."

"I'm planning to stay on for a week or so. I might as well make the most of the free trip." Allegra longed suddenly for comfortable companionship. "It would be fun to meet up."

"What about dinner tomorrow?"

"Lovely! Give me a call when you arrive."

"I'll do that," Rick said. "By the way, how did the Tempest interview go? Helena seemed all lit up about it."

Allegra gave a short laugh. "Let's just say it was hard work."

"I've heard he's quite a handful."

"That's an understatement. Anyway, I've spent a whole day trying to get him on paper. And now I'm just about to e-mail the article to Helena."

"Good for you! Until tomorrow, then. Look forward to seeing you, girl!"

The sound of a friendly voice had lifted Allegra.

Standing on her balcony overlooking the pool, she breathed in the salty, humid air and stretched her arms above her head to ease the stiffness in her shoulders. The brief nap hadn't helped much. Why was she making such heavy weather of this assignment? She had always had a facility with words and usually enjoyed the creative process of shaping her work. But this piece had been a nightmare.

She went back inside, took a long drink of water, and switched on her laptop. No more of this ridiculous shilly-shallying! She'd written the opening paragraph three times. Enough was enough! She read through the latest version quickly.

In a scene reminiscent of the opening sequence of the box-office hit Tycoon, *I stand on the deck of the sloop* Miranda *and admire her canvas and sleek lines. The helmsman has silver-gray eyes and windswept black hair, and wears an expression on his bronzed face that announces his element is the sea. Max Tempest has no time for landlubbers . . .*

She had tried desperately hard to be fair—to write without prejudice, without any attempt to flatter. But the piece lacked something intangible—like a jigsaw puzzle with one vital piece missing. She had managed to capture many of the real-life roles Max played: Max the actor, Max the sailor, Max the employer, Max the jealous guardian of his privacy. But his most important role—Max the caring human being and the sole relative of a lonely small boy—was, as she had promised, left unsaid.

Would Helena pick up on it? Hopefully not. The piece was well written and entertaining enough to satisfy readers, and she would be impressed by the account (edited, of course!) of the trip in *Miranda*. It would have to do. Allegra sighed. If she'd really wanted to get under Max Tempest's skin, she should have put aside her private feelings and refused to pay lip service to his demands. It was too late now. She had given him her word. There was nothing to do but get the piece finished and be done with it once and for all. And yet some utterly illogical part of her—wishful thinking, perhaps—told her that she hadn't seen the last of the man against whom, she now realized, the other men in her life had been measured and found wanting. Would she ever be truly free of him? And more to the point, did she really want to be?

That night Allegra slept badly. In her dreams she was being pursued down a dark street by a redheaded Irishman with Max's face. The faster she ran, the longer the street appeared, and she woke, perspiring and frightened, just as escape seemed impossible.

She lay among her twisted, crumpled sheets for a few minutes, staring at the ceiling until her rational mind took over. Her work was done! She no longer had to wrestle with it, and she was now as free as a bird. The week stretched ahead, filled with possibilities. She could sit back and congratulate herself on a job well done and be happy.

The most brilliant thing was that she was here in the United States. And now that her mother had gone to live in Spain, Allegra felt it was time to explore the possibility of spending more time getting to know the country her father had loved. It should be reasonably easy to transfer to a job in *Elegance's* New York office. And she intended to discuss this with Helena on her return. She would miss her family and her friends in London, but there were relatives here she needed to get to know. There was a whole new world to be explored, and she intended to make the most of it.

Allegra sighed. If everything was so wonderful, why was she feeling as if she had just lost something precious and irreplaceable? And why was she already thinking about the possibility of seeing Max Tempest one more time? She was fairly sure that if she picked up the phone. . . . No! Horrified, she leaped out of bed.

These ridiculous, leftover feelings she had for Max, she told herself as she flung herself into the shower, were dangerous. It would be a fatal mistake to imagine that a few casual kisses meant anything more than casual affection—a kind of token memory of the past. *Max is not just out of my league,* she reminded herself. *More like out of my universe.* How on earth could an ordinary working girl fit into his glamorous world? Seven years ago, the prospects of spending her life with Max had been far more realistic. In those days, he'd been a struggling young actor, and perhaps, if she'd been honest with him from the start, she might have gone with him to Hollywood and shared his life. But it was no use harking back to the past. What was done was done, and now it was too late. Max Tempest would never be more than a subject to interview—a star that was way out of her firmament.

She sighed. Perhaps she really ought to leave Cedar Bay while her heart, at least, was intact. Out of sight, out of mind. Once she had left this place, her brief encounter with Max would fade into an uncomfortable memory she could quickly put aside. She'd have dinner with Rick this evening as she'd promised and then head for Miami and the Everglades. She'd always wanted to explore them, and there was no time like the present.

Allegra spent a pleasant hour or so browsing through the souvenir shops around the marina that morning. Busy with her purchases, which included several items she would probably regret later when she tried to fit them into her suitcase, she was feeling relaxed and tranquil for the first time since arriving in Florida.

It was while she was making a selection from the rather garish array of postcards on a display stand on the quay that she felt a tug at her elbow and turned quickly. Her eyes widened at the sight of the small figure standing close behind her.

"Jack? Heavens! This is a nice surprise!"

She looked around. There was no sign of Max or Carlos, and the wide blue eyes were gazing up at her with a mixture of relief and apprehension.

She took his hand. "You're not on your own, are you?"

"I came on the boat with Carlos."

"I see." Allegra glanced around. "So, where is he?"

"I don't know. I've been looking for him. I got kind of lost."

Allegra heard the anxiety in his voice and put down the postcards. Carlos, she thought, must now be frantic.

"Don't worry," she said reassuringly, "we'll find him. He can't be far away. I expect he's looking everywhere for you too."

Jack shot her a guilty look. "Uh-uh." He shook his head. "He doesn't know I'm here."

Allegra looked alarmed. "Really?"

"I was hiding in the cabin."

Comprehension dawning, she tried not to laugh at his sheepish expression. "You mean you're a stowaway?"

Jack sighed, staring at his battered sneakers with furious concentration. "I got into the boat when Carlos wasn't looking. I thought it would be so fun to come over here. So, when the boat started, I hid in the cabin. I was gonna jump out at him . . ."

"And?"

Jack nodded. "When the engine stopped, I went up on deck, but Carlos had gone. He was a really long time."

"So you went looking for him?"

"Kind of. Then I saw you looking at the postcards. And I thought. . . ." He looked at her tentatively. "Maybe you'd help?"

"Of course I'll help." Allegra put out a hand and ruffled his thick black hair. He was such a woebegone little figure with his grubby face and the enormous bandage on his wrist. "How's the arm coming along, by the way?"

Jack looked at the strapping proudly. "It still hurts. Well, a little, anyway. I have to keep the dressing on."

"Of course," Allegra said seriously. "Well, we'd better find Carlos and get you back to the island—hopefully before your uncle notices you've gone."

Jack's lower lip protruded. "But can't I stay here with you for a while?"

Allegra shook her head firmly. "I'd love you to, Jack. I'd really enjoy some company. But we mustn't worry your uncle. We need to go back to the boat to find Carlos."

Jack looked disappointed. "But I could stay a while." The blue eyes pleaded with her. "Please?"

"Not until we let your uncle know where you are."

Ignoring his blandishments, she led the reluctant little boy down to the marina. When Max discovered that his nephew had disappeared, he would be frantic.

But there was no sign of the motor launch at her mooring. At Pier 75, there was just a stretch of clear blue water. They stared at each other.

"Wow!" said Jack, impressed.

"Wow, indeed." Allegra looked down at her small companion ruefully. "Now what do we do?"

Chapter Seven

Getting Jack back to the island wasn't, Allegra discovered, as simple as it would appear. There were no small boats available immediately for hire, and, when she tried calling Max to reassure him that his nephew was safe, he wasn't answering his cell phone. She left a message and tried calling the house, but no one picked up the phone there either. That probably meant that everyone must be out searching for the little boy. She could only imagine what they must be feeling.

"I'm hungry." Jack, now safe in adult company, was quite unconcerned. He had spied the hot dog stand near the jetty, and Allegra decided she might as well treat her unexpected visitor to lunch while they waited for a boat.

Allegra watched him as he devoured hot dogs and a chocolate milk shake. She couldn't blame Max for being so protective of the boy.

"It'll be okay," Jack said, misinterpreting her thoughtful expression. "Max might not even notice I'm not there." He threw a piece of his bun to a predatory pelican swooping down over the water.

"Maybe not." But Allegra thought it highly unlikely. Heaven knew what he might think when he realized Jack was gone. Hopefully, he'd picked up her message.

"Maria might be mad with me, I guess. I was supposed to play by the pool until Carlos got back."

"Maria?"

"She's Carlos' wife. I like her a lot." He looked wistful. "If I could live here with my uncle, she'd take care of me." He frowned, pushing out his bottom lip. "I hate New York."

"Really?"

"I miss my mom." The blue eyes were wistful. "She'd want me to be here with Max, don't you think?"

Allegra, with her heart aching at the look on the child's face, searched desperately for the right things to say.

"Of course. But what about the kind people who look after you?"

"They wouldn't mind. They have other kids to take care of as well as me." He sighed. "I asked Max if I could live here with him, but he just said, 'We'll see.' And when people say that, they usually mean no."

"You think so?" Allegra restrained herself from putting her arms around him.

He wiped his ketchup-covered fingers thoughtfully. "I just hope," he said, "he won't be too mad at me when he finds out why I'm here."

"He'll just be happy to know you're safe."

Jack shrugged. "Once when I went to a zoo with my mom, I got lost. And when she found me, she yelled."

"Adults get scared, Jack. And that's why they get angry."

But Jack did not look convinced. It took a chocolate milk shake to put the smile back on his face.

"Thanks," he said. "Do they have chocolate shakes in London?"

"Oh, yes."

"Cool! Maybe, I'll come visit you someday?"

"I'd really like that!"

Forty minutes later, as they sped across the sun-spangled water toward the island with Allegra at the helm, Jack's grubby, small face began to take on an anxious look.

"Don't worry. I'm not going anywhere until I've explained everything," Allegra said as they nosed against the jetty.

She took Jack's hand as they trudged across the beach, making for the steps. The sun at midday was pitiless, and it was a relief to reach the shelter of the pines. They had not even begun the steep upward climb when Max, wearing nothing but a pair of faded denim shorts, appeared from nowhere with Carlos hard on his heels. They must have seen the boat, Allegra realized, and come running.

Max's face was alight, first with relief and then, predictably, with anger.

"Jack! Where did you go?" He squatted down in

front of his nephew and grabbed him by the shoulders. "Are you okay?"

Jack glanced at Allegra, and she squeezed his shoulder. "He's fine."

"Where did you find him?" Max demanded. "I've been out of my mind with worry."

"He found me, actually." Allegra winked at Jack reassuringly. "It was just a joke that went wrong. Jack hid on the boat this morning before Carlos set off."

Max stood up slowly, uncoiling his lean, bronzed body, and looked from one to the other. "He did what?"

"It was gonna be a surprise." Jack suddenly found his tongue. He looked up sheepishly at Carlos, who turned away, hiding a grin. "But he went away, and then I couldn't find him."

"I just happened to be on the quayside," Allegra said. "I tried to call you, Max, but you didn't pick up your cell phone."

Max shook his head slowly. "Must have left it in my shirt pocket."

"We had hot dogs for lunch," Jack said defiantly. "And a chocolate shake. While we waited for a boat."

Max was still bristling.

"Don't ever play a trick like that again," he said sternly. "Understand? It was a stupid, thoughtless thing to do. Go up to the house and go to your room. I'll talk to you later."

"Can Allegra come?"

"Do as I say," Max said. "Now!"

Jack looked at Allegra wistfully. "Thanks," he said, "I had fun."

He followed Carlos up the steps, where Maria was waiting for them, his small shoulders hunched in dejection as they disappeared between the trees.

Allegra restrained her impulse to run after him for a hug. Instead, she glared at Max accusingly.

"He didn't mean to worry you. He was searching for Carlos when he found me."

"And if he hadn't?" Max retorted. "Anything could have happened."

"But it didn't. Fortunately."

"We searched the whole island—Maria came and helped. We were going crazy! He could have drowned for all I knew!" His voice was ragged with emotion. Then, recovering with an effort, he gave her a rueful look. "You'd better come on up to the house and let me get you a cold drink."

"Thanks," Allegra said stiffly, "but I have to get back. Look, I hope you won't be too hard on Jack. It was just the usual kind of mischief small boys get up to."

Max looked grim. "He won't be trying that little game again!"

"I'm sure you're right. But then," she said, her eyes challenging him, "that's rather up to you, isn't it?"

"What's that supposed to mean?"

"Children only get up to mischief when they're bored. Maybe he needs more of your attention."

Max eyed her coldly. "Okay," he said in an irritating drawl. "So now you're an expert on child psychology as well as journalism."

The sarcasm in his voice made her flinch. "It's common sense," she said bluntly. "You told me yourself you hardly know him. It's a miracle he's as balanced as he appears to be."

"Is that so?" His voice was cold, anger vibrating just below the surface. "And what makes you think you're qualified to pass judgment?"

The blue eyes flashed angrily. "It's not exactly rocket science. Jack needs a father figure—not some robot going through the motions for the sake of appearances."

Max stared at her for a moment. Then, he gave a sudden, harsh bark of laughter—the kind of laughter that contained no humor—merely a kind of amazed disbelief.

"You really have quite an opinion of me, don't you? Yesterday, an unscrupulous womanizer; today, inhuman."

Allegra shrugged. "I'm only concerned for Jack. But don't pay any attention to me. When you're tired of your latest role as guardian, just send your nephew back to New York and forget all about him. After all, no one can say you haven't taken an interest in him. Not bad going—a few weeks vacation in seven years."

In the silence, Max looked at her through narrowed eyes. "I think you'd better leave."

"Don't worry. I'm going," Allegra retorted. "And if it doesn't offend your dignity, please say good-bye to Jack for me. You've no idea how lucky you are to have him."

She was halfway across the bay before her anger began to subside. She'd gone, perhaps a little too far. Her advice had been kindly meant, but Max's reaction had infuriated her. Still, his relationship with Jack was really none of her business, and her critical remarks had been ill timed. No wonder he had gone on the defense. She should have kept her mouth firmly shut.

By the time she had reached the hotel, she was feeling rather ashamed of herself. Until she suddenly remembered that, despite the trouble she had taken to rescue Jack that morning, his uncle hadn't uttered a single word of thanks for her pains.

"You look amazing, girl!" Rick held her at arm's length, his eyes full of admiration.

Allegra was wearing white silk trousers and an emerald top, which enhanced her newly acquired tan.

"You're looking pretty good yourself," she said, laughing. His face was tanned, his shock of fair hair bleached almost white by the sun.

"Tonight," he informed her, "the sky's the limit. I happen to know a guy who was able to get me a table in the best restaurant in town!"

Rick was not exaggerating. Allegra found herself being ushered to a table in a softly lit alcove in the kind of restaurant patronized only by the wealthy and privileged. It was small—scarcely more than a dozen tables positioned to provide the ultimate in intimate dining. The flowers exquisitely arranged on each table were real, the heavy damask tablecloths were white as the driven snow, and the array of silver and crystal gleamed softly under the glowing lamps.

Other couples dining were placed so discreetly that you were only aware of their presence by the soft clink of glasses and cutlery and the murmured attentions of the waiter.

"This looks like the kind of place you need to book six months in advance," Allegra said, smiling across the table.

"Contacts." Rick winked at her. "That's all you need!"

They ordered swordfish in an aromatic sauce after serious contemplation of the exotic menu, and for the first time since she had arrived in Florida, Allegra at last began to relax. The food was superb and Rick was excellent company, entertaining her with tales of his exploits in Miami.

"Tonight has been fun," she said as they waited for coffee.

"Then maybe we should do this again?" Rick smiled. "Why not come down to the Keys with me for a couple of days? You could do some sightseeing while I'm working."

Allegra wasn't even tempted. Rick was great company, but she had never felt remotely attracted to him. Unfortunately, there was only one man who could still send her pulse into overdrive and stretch her nerves to the breaking point.

She shook her head. "Thanks, but I already have plans." She smiled to take the sting out of her refusal, and then, over his shoulder, she caught a glimpse of a couple leaving their table in a screened alcove across the room. The waiter was hovering solicitously, ushering them with obvious deference toward the door. The smile died on her lips, and she froze as she saw why.

It was Max, accompanied by a tall, fashionably skinny, dark-haired girl whose face was strangely familiar. Of course. Daria Cavendish. The latest catwalk sensation.

She had made the cover page of *Elegance* quite recently. She was very young to have made it so effortlessly to the top, but her manner and looks said it all.

Allegra's breath caught in her throat, and her heart was suddenly gripped by something fierce and possessive. Afterward she was extremely grateful that she had seen them first. At least she'd had a second or two to gather her wits and replace the expression of chagrin on her face with something less obvious.

They made an extraordinarily handsome couple, of course, Max in a silver-gray lightweight suit, the collarless blue shirt emphasizing the heavy tan; and Daria, in black, undeniably striking in that gaunt, high-cheekboned English way, with her long, red-tipped fingers resting in the crook of Max's arm.

Rick, noticing Allegra's involuntary reaction, glanced over his shoulder quickly, and it was at this precise moment Max saw them. His reaction was not as marked as Allegra's—he was much too good an actor to give it away—but his surprise showed on his face momentarily—quickly replaced by a mask of cool politeness, the gray eyes like chips of ice.

He nodded. "Allegra."

She had never longed so much for the earth to swallow her up. Rick's eyes, she knew, were fixed on her face, watching every nuance of expression. The sight of Max advancing toward their table had brought a rush of blood to her face that had quickly receded, leaving her marble-pale. She was trapped—there was no escaping the situation, and she knew it.

Somehow, she forced a smile. "Hello, Max," she said calmly. "You're the last person I expected to run into."

Rick, pushing back his chair, rose to his feet, and the awkward introductions were made.

"So you're Max's journalist," Daria said, her high, childish voice strangely at odds with her sophisticated appearance. "I hope you've written nice things about him?"

Allegra smiled glacially. "I've done my best to."

Max was looking at Rick.

"On vacation here?"

"Actually, no. I've been on an assignment in Clearwater. I'm leaving tomorrow for the Keys."

"Rick's a photographer. We're old friends," Allegra explained, and Max's eyes hardened.

"Is that so?"

Allegra bit her lip. The acerbic tone probably meant that Max thought she and Rick were somehow collaborating on her story. If he thought that the photographer had been nosing around the island hoping to get some close-ups, he was making the wrong connections.

"Will you join us for a drink?" Rick asked casually, seemingly unaware of the hostility in Max's expression.

"Thanks, but I try to avoid fraternizing with the press," he said coldly. "Don't let us interrupt your evening." Before turning to the door, he threw Allegra a sharp look. "Good night."

The fun had gone out of the evening. Allegra knew that even before the door had closed behind them. And Rick, obviously annoyed by Max's churlish dismissal, stared at Allegra's flushed face.

"You blushed! I didn't know women did that anymore."

"The man just gets under my skin, that's all," Allegra muttered. The sight of Max with another woman was far more painful than she was willing to admit . . .

Rick shrugged. "I didn't know he was Daria Cavendish's latest squeeze. She looks a lot more impressive airbrushed, she does. But then that sort of emaciated type has never rung my bell. Wouldn't have thought she was Tempest's type either. She can't be more than eighteen or nineteen!"

"I wouldn't know," Allegra said stiffly. Once, age difference had been an issue with Max. She'd found that out the hard way. But of course, if she'd been as sophisticated as Daria seven years ago, things might have been very different.

Unable to finish her liqueur despite Rick's urging, she was grateful to go out into the soft night air. As they walked slowly back to the hotel, Allegra, only half listening to Rick's cheerful ramblings found herself longing to be alone.

"Thanks for a great evening, Rick," she said as they reached the foyer. "The food was wonderful, and I really enjoyed seeing you again."

For a second, he looked disappointed. Then he smiled and took both her hands. "If you change your mind about the trip to Key West, I'm at the Miramar on South Twenty-third. Give me a call. I don't leave till Tuesday."

He suddenly leaned forward to kiss her, and Allegra stiffened and offered her cheek.

"Thanks again," she whispered and escaped with a sigh of relief into the brightly lit lobby.

An evening ruined by Max, she thought as she went toward the elevators. It was such a coincidence that he should have chosen the same venue to entertain his latest conquest—although judging by the ambience, it was probably *the* place to dine. The sight of him with another woman still had power to affect her—that was painfully obvious. *You're a sad case, Allegra Howard,* she told herself as she reached forward to press the call button. And then, hand in midair, she froze at the sound of her name.

"Allow me." Max jabbed the button as she whirled around to face him.

"That was a very touching good-bye." he said, smiling coldly. "I fully expected your friend to go inside with you."

"Why are you following me?" she demanded, her voice uneven.

"I need to talk to you." And as the elevator doors opened, he stepped in with her. "Which floor?"

Allegra checked a sudden, crazy desire to rush out again into the foyer.

"Five," she said through clenched teeth. The confined space imposed an intimacy that made it impossible for Allegra to disguise her discomfiture. The handsome face was impassive as he stood facing her, his arms folded across his chest like some hostile interrogator. She tried to concentrate on a place just to the left of Max's right ear. When the doors opened, she marched ahead down the corridor, holding herself rigidly.

"I have no idea what you want with me," she snapped,

fumbling with her key card, "but it's late, I'm extremely tired, and I have nothing to say to you."

Max took the card from her hand. "But I have something to say to you," he said coldly, "and for obvious reasons, I'd prefer not to say it in the corridor."

Allegra stood with her back to the door. "I'm afraid you'll have to. There's no way I'm letting you in."

"Don't be ridiculous! Believe me," he said, 'I have absolutely no designs on your honor. There's something I want to ask you, that's all."

"And if I don't want to answer?"

"Allegra," he said, and the quiet, patient tone was at variance with the look in his steely eyes. "I don't want to create a public scene, but if you go on like this, I guarantee results. Can you imagine what the tabloids would make of it? Might not go down too well with your editor, huh?"

Allegra gritted her teeth but moved aside, allowing him to open the door and flick on the lights. Inside, she stood staring at him, her arms wrapped around her body defensively, her eyes sparkling with indignation.

"Aren't you at least going to offer me a nightcap?" He gave a wry grin. "A little hospitality might go a long way."

"I've already told you I'm very tired," she snapped. "So whatever you need to say, please do so."

"Fine." Max sat down in the armchair near the window and crossed one long leg over the other. "I'll get straight to the point. This Rick—the suddenly acquired photographer friend you kindly introduced to me tonight."

"Yes?" Allegra threw her handbag on to the dressing

table and looked across at Max coldly. "What about him?"

"I'd like to know more about him. Quite a bit more, actually."

"Really? Why? Perhaps you would like me to show similar interest in your dinner date?"

Max's lip curled. "Don't try and play mind games with me, Allegra. Rick Fielding is a photojournalist, and I want to know what he's doing here with you."

Allegra stared at Max woodenly. Suddenly she liked the idea of making him suffer. Why shouldn't she? She was still smarting after that unpleasant little confrontation in the restaurant.

"I believe he told you. He's working here on an assignment."

"Which is?"

"None of your business, Max. Perhaps you should ask him yourself. I can tell you where he's staying if you like."

"Don't get clever with me, Allegra," he warned, his body stiffening. "You know how I feel about journalists."

"You're paranoid about them, yes."

"Paranoid? I don't think so. Why wouldn't I sit up and take notice? You're the first journalist I've ever allowed anywhere near me for a very long time. And now, surprise, surprise, one of your photographer friends appears from nowhere. Interesting, isn't it, how he just happened to be dining with you at Armando's tonight?" He raised a scornful eyebrow. "So, tell me, what am I supposed to think?"

Allegra leaned back against the door, eyeing him

coldly. Part of her was enjoying this, savoring the fact that for once, she had Max Tempest on the back foot. And she was in no hurry to ease the pressure.

"Think what you like. Why shouldn't Rick and I enjoy a meal at a good restaurant? Armando's has an excellent reputation, and it certainly lived up to it tonight."

"And also," Max informed her, "it's not exactly the kind of place where you'd find a guy like Fielding. Unless it was worth his while to be there."

Allegra took one look at the intense expression on Max's face and began to laugh. "Do you know how patronizing that sounds? We live in London, remember? You can find a restaurant like Armando's on every street corner."

Max had the grace to look embarrassed. "That's not what I meant . . ."

"You really believe I would set you up? Just who do you think you are, Max? Do you honestly imagine anyone would go to that much trouble?"

"Maybe not," he growled, running a nervous hand through his hair. "I don't give two hoots about myself. But I worry about Jack."

Allegra sighed. She knew she was behaving badly. Deliberately goading him because of her own feelings of jealous spite. The sight of him standing in the restaurant with Daria Cavendish's possessive arm through his had been hard to take. But suddenly her desire to hurt seemed petty.

"Oh, for heaven's sake!" she said. "Relax. Rick's arrival here is pure coincidence. He's working on a book on deep sea fishing. And he's leaving shortly for Key West."

Max's mouth relaxed, but he went on staring at her, half in doubt.

"He's not interested in you," Allegra continued. "Rick's not one of the paparazzi, I can assure you. And I had no idea he was in Florida until yesterday."

He believed her. That was clear. But the look he gave her was tinged with resentment.

"How well you do know him?" he demanded.

"Well enough," she said irritably. "If you must know, we used to work together." The wicked desire to provoke him overtook her again. "Actually, I'm thinking about going down to Key West with him for a few days."

If Allegra had slapped his face, Max's reaction could not have been more pronounced.

"You're doing what?"

Allegra shrugged. "It might be fun. Why not?"

"I wouldn't have thought that was your style."

"And what makes you think you're an expert on the subject? You know nothing about me."

"That's not strictly true. I may be a little out of date, perhaps. But the last couple of days have brought me more or less up to speed."

Too late, Allegra saw him glance at the neat stack of printer paper on the table. She always liked to proofread her work from hard copy. Max had picked it up before Allegra had time to protest. Her heart was hammering absurdly as she marched across the room and held out her hand.

"Do you mind? That's private."

Max laughed. Now it was his turn to be in control, and he intended to enjoy every minute of it.

"Private? How can you say that about something that is about to be read by thousands of your readers?"

Allegra's eyes blazed. "You know what I mean. It's my work, and you have no right to read it before publication. In fact, it's not even ethical." She tried to snatch the paper out of his hand, but he held it out of her reach with a provoking smile.

"I have every right to read what you've written about me." He shook his head in mock disapproval. "It can't be as bad as that, surely!"

"Please!" She held her hand out again, and her voice was harsh with frustration. "I'm serious, Max."

"So am I!" He laughed as, even more incensed, she made another desperate lunge. This time, as he jerked the paper out of her reach, she snatched at thin air, lost her balance on her high-heeled sandals, and fell, literally, into his arms.

"Easy!" he muttered into her hair.

Allegra's heart was beating very fast and light, her murmur of protest a mere whisper, and she stayed where she was for a few seconds, cradled against his chest. The thrill of feeling his arms holding her swept through her entire body, leaving her confused and dizzy. She raised her head, and the look he gave her threatened every rational, sane thought in her mind, making her feel wholly, utterly female. She wanted the moment to last forever.

"Steady!" he admonished her gravely. "Women do,

occasionally, fling themselves at me but not quite so blatantly!"

Suddenly, Allegra was seventeen again—gauche, shy, defenseless. But only for a moment. Quick to recover her poise, she treated him to a long, cold, contemptuous stare.

"Get over yourself, Max," she said cuttingly. "And if you really want to, go ahead and read what I've written about you. I can't say I much enjoyed the task."

"That's too bad. Does that mean I would enjoy reading it even less?"

She went to the icebox, poured herself a glass of water, and dropped into the chair opposite. "See for yourself," she said disdainfully.

Suddenly, he was laughing at her. "It's surprisingly easy to get that temper of yours fired up." Carefully, he straightened out the untidy pile of paper. He put it facedown on the table with the look of a man who had won his round after a hard contest. "These days, I make a point of never reading anything written about me by the press, so relax!"

Chapter Eight

Allegra had rarely felt so angry and so vulnerable as she sat there in silence, staring at Max. His reaction to the content of the piece wouldn't have bothered her. She had been scrupulously honest—without the slightest attempt to flatter her subject—and if Max had found her view of him less than complimentary, that would have been his problem. But it had been a shock to discover just how much his opinion of her writing mattered to her, and her panic must have reflected that. He had made a fool of her, and she was furious.

He regarded her flushed face thoughtfully. "I suppose it serves me right."

"Sorry?"

She was trying hard to conceal her anger and embarrassment, but the defiant glance she threw in his direction probably hadn't fooled him.

"Oh, I'd guess it's all very subtle," he said. "And

130

beautifully written of course. But I'm kind of convinced that if I read this article about a stranger, I wouldn't much care for the guy."

She shrugged a little too elaborately. "Think what you like. What I wrote was fair. Objective. Impartial."

"Sure. And I bet you haven't missed a thing—background, career, lifestyle. You're right. Except that you've probably described a man without feeling. Talented. successful—and emotionally an iceberg!"

"What did you expect? You gave me so little to go on! In fact, you ruled out the things that make you human. This deep-seated dislike of the press . . ."

"I'd have no problem with them if they stopped trying to infiltrate my private life," he said.

"You're referring to me?"

Suddenly, she was tired of all the verbal skirmishing.

"No," he said, "of course not."

She looked at him, taken aback by the sudden gentleness of his tone.

"You've been fighting me ever since you arrived in Florida." His voice was ragged with emotion. "Isn't it time we called a truce?"

She was edgy, fearful even. She put down her glass with a slightly unsteady hand as she got to her feet. She needed to show him the door before the conversation became too personal.

"I'm really tired, Max. It's been a long day. Would you mind leaving now?" To her dismay there was a slight tremor in her voice—enough to make him leave his seat and move toward her.

"But we have unfinished business." He got to his

feet, took both her hands in his, and forced her to look at him. "What are you afraid of?"

"Nothing!" She shook her head stubbornly but she left her hands in his.

"Tonight," he said, "I wanted to knock Fielding down."

She frowned. "Why? I've already told you. He's just . . ."

"Not because he's a photographer." His voice was husky. "But because he was with you."

He raised her hand to his lips, and she met his look bravely enough. But then as he pressed her hand against his cheek, her eyes betrayed her once again. He was sure he could see the longing in them, the hunger that matched his own.

They stood there gazing at each other, and suddenly time stopped, then flipped into reverse. There she was. The woman he had fallen in love with the first time he'd set eyes on her. Nothing had changed—the corn-gold hair, the satin sheen of her skin, the clear blue gaze, the fragrance of her. His golden girl. Would she believe him if he told her how she made him feel? There was only one way to find out: Tell her the simple truth.

"Would you believe me if I told you I feel the same about you now as I did all that time ago?"

She stiffened, snatching her hand from his, and her eyes went blank.

"No!" she said, and walked to the door.

He'd blown it. Her body language, the look of shock on her face, said it all. She'd reacted as if he had insulted her, had been repelled by his words as if they'd been nothing but a barefaced come-on.

"Why?"

"Because I won't be seduced by words, Max."

She meant it. The tremor had gone from her voice and by the expression on her face, she felt nothing but contempt for him. She thought he was hitting on her. And in fairness, wasn't he? Of course he wanted her. But there was more, much more to it than that.

Max took a deep breath and steadied himself. What did he think he was doing? How exactly would a woman like Allegra fit into his plans? So much had changed since his sister had died. Jack was his priority now, and nothing could be allowed to interfere with that. It was time he pulled himself together and made a dignified exit.

She had opened the door and stood waiting, wooden-faced. There was nowhere to go from here, and he knew it.

He shrugged, joining her in the doorway, and she turned her head, not looking at him but at a point just to the right of his chin.

The corner of his mouth quirked ruefully. "Good night, Allegra."

Leaning forward, he put his hands lightly on her shoulders, kissed her cheek, and walked down the corridor to the elevators.

Allegra closed the door with an audible sigh and leaned her back against it. Oh, dear Lord. What a performance she'd given! "I won't be seduced by words, Max!" She repeated her words, mocking herself in a high, affected voice. No wonder he had given her that compassionate smile before he left. She'd acted like some prim Victorian governess resisting the advances of an importunate lover.

It took a second or two before her eyes focused on his jacket, lying where he had left it at the bottom of her bed. Instinctively, she went to pick it up, holding it against her, breathing in the scent of him, savoring the subtle trace of cologne and expensive soap and leather, pressing her cheek against the fine cloth. Every female instinct in her body quivered to life, and she sat down on the edge of the bed, suddenly weak with longing.

Who exactly did she think she was kidding? Certainly not herself. And not Max either. He must have known it was all an act. What woman in her right mind would be crazy enough to reject a man like Max Tempest? And that was what she had done! Not because she was still carrying the vestiges of hurt pride and wounded vanity. Not because she saw it as payback for the misery he had inflicted on her seven years ago. It was a lot simpler than that. After all this time, she was still in love with him.

She'd realized that the minute she'd seen him with Daria Cavendish. Saw the possessive hand holding his arm. Sensed the affection between them, the easy camaraderie. It had been almost like the sensation of blood returning to a numbed limb, hot, painful, prickling through her veins, bringing her to life again, forcing her to face the uncomfortable truth.

She had always known, deep down, that she would never feel about any other man as she felt about Max. And that was why she couldn't let him near her—mentally or physically. She closed her eyes, remembering the look of intensity on his face as he said the words that told her everything. He said he felt the same as he had all those years ago. So why didn't she believe him?' Because she wasn't seventeen anymore. She didn't want lust. She wanted love. Max couldn't give her that, and common sense told her that she couldn't settle for anything less.

The shrill ring of the phone jolted her across the room. Max! It had to be! He'd remembered his jacket! Suddenly, all her brave determination vanished at the thought of him.

She snatched the phone with shaking hands.

"Allegra? Sorry, were you fast asleep? My dear, I just had to ring to congratulate you on your piece. I'm impressed! Well done."

For a second or two, Allegra was speechless. Struggling to get hold of herself as the disappointment hit her, she reminded herself that this was her boss and that she had better pull herself together. Fast.

She took a firmer grip on the phone and cleared her throat. "Helena! Good to hear from you! I'm glad you approve. And no, I wasn't asleep. I met up with Rick Fielding, and we had dinner. I . . . I've just got back."

"So, he managed to catch up with you! Good! You deserve some fun. Now, about the Tempest piece."

"Yes?" Allegra gripped the receiver tightly. She knew what was coming. With Helena it was impossible to get it absolutely right.

"I was rather hoping you'd have managed to dig up something about the man's love life. Just to spice the story up? I suppose that there's no truth to the rumor that Daria Cavendish is his latest squeeze?"

Allegra hoped her sharp intake of breath wasn't audible over the phone. "He wouldn't budge on his private life, I'm afraid."

"A pity. Still, it can't be helped, and as I said, it's a very good piece," Helena said briskly. "Well, I'd better let you get some sleep! It's seven A.M. here and pouring rain! Enjoy the sunshine, won't you? I've got work to do!"

So typical of her to add the last little barb, Allegra thought. As if the interview in Florida hadn't been Helena's idea! Now, more than ever, she wished she'd had the courage to refuse the Tempest job. She should have started running in the opposite direction immediately after Max's name had been mentioned.

That piece of gossip about Daria and Max couldn't have come at a more propitious time. Helena's source was obviously right. So, they were clearly involved—which made Max's overtures tonight even more reprehensible.

To think that only minutes ago she had felt herself weakening! If that had been Max on the phone, she had no doubt whatsoever what would have happened next.

She'd had a lucky escape, she thought, as she kicked off her sandals and slipped her dress over her head. She could walk away unscathed with her heart intact. So, why, in that case, did it feel as if a bright light had suddenly been switched off? As if she had walked out of the sun into a cold dark place?

Forget it! And forget Max Tempest! In London, she had a life waiting for her.

She took the jacket and hung it in the back of her

wardrobe. It could stay there forever as far as she was concerned!

Leaving, Max knew, had been the only option. Walking away before the whole thing with Allegra became too hot too handle.

He could have stayed, been honest with her, explained exactly what was going on in his life—why it had become so complicated—told her about his plans for Jack. But then what? He had nothing to offer her but the problems he was wrestling with. And if he wanted to achieve his aims, he needed to do it without further complications. To get custody of his nephew, he had to be completely single-minded, with nothing going on in his life that might complicate matters.

Take today. He should have kept his eye on the ball—should never have allowed the little guy to get on that boat! The mere thought of losing him brought a lump to his throat. Anything could have happened to him if it hadn't been for Allegra. And afterward, when he had gone to talk to him, he had felt like a complete heel.

"Are you gonna send me back to the foster home?" Jack's face, as he gazed up at him, had broken his heart.

"No. I'm not going to do that." He had put his arms around the small figure and given him a bear hug.

"Promise?"

"Sure. Just don't give me any more scares, okay? Stay close."

Max ran a hand through his hair. He'd thought he had it all worked out and under control. And he had. Until Allegra had walked back into his life.

The image of her at seventeen still haunted him, heart-breakingly young, sweet, vulnerable, on the threshold of womanhood. And now?

Tonight those expressive eyes had acknowledged him. The sweet mouth that promised him paradise was his for the taking, however fiercely she had tried to deny it. She had always been there, just out of focus—a part of him he couldn't let go. And there was nothing he could do to change that—even if he wanted to.

"You enjoy your evening, Señor Max?"

Carlos' sharp eyes caught the grim expression on Max's face as he stepped into the boat.

He grinned savagely. "I've had better."

They were halfway across the bay when he remembered where he'd left his jacket.

"Good morning," Rick said. "Thought I'd check on you to see if you were okay after last night."

Allegra, finishing breakfast on the terrace, stared at him, puzzled.

"Why on earth shouldn't I be?" she demanded. It was eight A.M., for heaven's sake! Just a bit early for a social call! Sleep had eluded her until the wee hours, and she felt irritable at the mere sight of Rick's cheerful face.

"Your visitor," he insisted. "I saw him follow you into the lift. You didn't look too happy about it."

Allegra colored. "Didn't I?" She forced herself to sound casual. "Well, actually, it was rather late to be answering questions about my article."

"You're joking!" Rick sat down and made signs to the waitress to bring him coffee. "That's out of order—

although it doesn't surprise me. The man's an arrogant so-and-so. Did you see the way he looked at us in the restaurant last night?" He gave her a shrewd look. "Didn't outstay his welcome, did he?"

"He was a perfect gentleman and left after our discussion," Allegra said calmly. Rick had absolutely no right to question her about Max, and under different circumstances she would have told him so. But it wasn't a good idea to let him think she was rattled. Once a newshound, always a newshound. Rick could sniff out a story with the best of them, and she needed to put him off the scent.

"You're blushing again."

"You're sure it's not sunburn?" She forced a smile. "Oh, come on, Rick. I never mix business with pleasure. You know that!"

He grinned. "Don't I, though!" He gave her a wicked grin "And isn't it a crying shame!" He picked up an uneaten slice of toast from her plate and crunched it irritatingly. "I suppose you haven't changed your mind about Key West? It could be fun."

"Sorry, no. I've decided to check out tomorrow and head for Miami." She'd made up her mind to do that earlier. A few days sightseeing and then back to work and reality.

"That's a pity. I'd have enjoyed your company." Rick made a sad face but made no further efforts to persuade her.

"See you back in London," he said as he left. "And don't let Tempest bully you."

She didn't need telling. Once she had left Cedar Bay,

she knew there was no reason why their paths should ever cross again.

Of course, there was the matter of his jacket. Perhaps she should make an effort to get it back to him. Or maybe Max would come himself to fetch it. . . . *Oh, get a grip,* she told herself angrily. This kind of thinking isn't just weakness. It's insanity.

"Shouldn't you be taking a siesta? Don't you know it's crazy to sunbathe at this time of day?"

Max had brazenly demanded Allegra's cell phone number from Ed, and she was at the hotel pool when he called her.

The retrieval of his jacket had provided him with the perfect excuse to call, but suddenly, he had no desire to use such an obvious pretext. He'd been determined to see her again—he couldn't care less about the jacket— and it was ridiculous to pretend otherwise.

"Have you never heard of factor forty?" she asked him.

"Never use the stuff," he said. "But then, unlike mad dogs, Englishmen, and Allegra Howard, I usually stay out of the midday sun."

"Actually, I was just about to go indoors." She sounded cool, distant, and utterly in control. "What can I do for you, anyway?"

"I wondered," he plowed on rather clumsily, "if I'd catch you before your trip to Key West."

He heard the sharp intake of breath. "If you're on a fishing expedition, you're wasting your time."

"Guilty as charged." He laughed. "Right. Let me re-phrase that. Are you taking the trip with Fielding or not?"

"Actually, no. Not that it's any of your business."

"It's just that I wondered if you'd be able to fit in a sailing trip with Jack and me tomorrow morning?"

"What?" She sounded breathless. The abrupt directness of his approach had clearly thrown her completely.

He shrugged. "You know Jack's taken a shine to you. He'd kind of like to say good-bye properly. And we'd both like to thank you for rescuing him the other day." He paused briefly. "Carlos is leaving for Tampa tomorrow, but he could pick you up before he leaves. Could you make it over here by ten thirty?"

"Tomorrow?"

Had he blown it? She was surprised—shocked even—he could sense that. "You have plans?"

There was a brief pause. "No," she said hesitantly. "Tomorrow should be fine. Thank you."

Allegra went on sitting there with her phone clutched in her hand. She'd disguised her feelings well, she thought. He could not have guessed from her tone that at the sound of his voice her stomach had caved in, her resistance crumbling even before he had finished speaking.

What was it about the man that turned her into a "yes" woman?

She swallowed hard. She was such an idiot! Max was certainly living up to his reputation! Yesterday, Daria Cavendish. Tomorrow, Allegra Howard. And she, poor fool, was aiding and abetting him! How sad was that! Still, there was plenty of time to cancel. All she had to do was pick up the phone, tell him she couldn't make it, save herself a world of heartache. It was that simple.

But there had been something in his voice she hadn't heard before. An eagerness? A desire to please? Whatever it was, she'd found it irresistible.

She got slowly to her feet and gathered her things. Why not admit it? She could no more stay away from Max Tempest than a moth could resist a flame.

"Hi, Allegra!"

Jack was hopping with excitement at the sight of her the following morning and Maria, Carlos' pretty dark-eyed wife, greeted her with a shy smile before turning to adjust the little boy's collar and smoothe the dark hair back from his forehead.

"I will bring coffee, yes?" she asked Max.

Max looked at Allegra. "You'd like some?"

"I had a cup before leaving, thanks."

"Then we might as well get started."

Jack punched the air. "Yes!"

"Can you sail a boat?" he asked Allegra as they followed his uncle down the steps to the boathouse.

"I'm afraid not." She smiled. "I thought I'd just let you guys do all the work."

She was rewarded by a smile, which in a few years would flutter as many hearts as his uncle's.

They had almost reached the bottom of the steps when Max's cell phone rang.

"Darn it!" He looked for a second as if he might switch it off and then, frowning, changed his mind.

Allegra watched his face as he listened and saw his expression change from irritation to concern.

"When did this happen?" he demanded. "Right. Yes. Sure. I'll come as soon as I can. Thanks for letting me know."

He replaced his phone in his shirt pocket and ran a hand through his black hair distractedly. For a moment he stared from Jack to Allegra as if he'd forgotten who they were. And then, recovering with an effort, he lifted his hands in a gesture of helpless resignation.

"I guess the trip's off." He glanced at his watch. "I have to get to Clearwater as soon as possible."

Allegra looked at him sharply. "You're joking!"

Had he really had the temerity to drag her here—only to cancel at a minute's notice?

"I'm sorry," he said curtly. "It's unavoidable."

Jack's face had crumpled. "But you said . . ." he groaned. "You promised."

"Jack." Max's voice was firm but gentle. "I'm really sorry I have to disappoint you. I was looking forward to the trip too." He turned to Allegra, who was having difficulty keeping her face expressionless. "I wouldn't cancel unless it was absolutely necessary."

"It's not fair!"

Allegra looked at Jack's disappointed face. Didn't Max know how important it was to keep a promise to a child?

"I'm really sorry." Max began to lead the way up the steps. "It can't be helped. We'll go another time."

Jack's lower lip stuck out mutinously as he followed unwillingly in his uncle's wake. "But why can't we go today?"

"We just can't," Max informed him flatly. "And that's all there is to it. Come on, Jack! Don't give me a hard time."

"Listen," Allegra said, "it's a shame we can't go sailing. But since your uncle Max is busy, we could still do something together. I have no other plans, and I'd really like to spend the day with you." She glanced up coolly at Max. "If that's all right with you?"

Max looked amazed. "You're sure?"

"Jack and I could go to the beach. Perhaps Maria could fix us a picnic." She looked at Jack. "Shall we do that?"

Jack hesitated and looked at his bandage. "But I can't go swimming."

"No, but we could shrimp and catch crabs and play ball."

He nodded, his small face brightening. "Okay. I'll go fetch the shrimping nets."

Max watched him run across the terrace and shook his head in wonder. "I wish I knew how to handle kids like that. You obviously have the magic touch."

"Just common sense." Allegra was still annoyed at the way Max had coolly altered his plans without the slightest regard for hers.

"It's good of you to do this." His voice was gruff, tinged with embarrassment. "I seem to spend a lot of time being grateful to you. But it would help since Carlos won't be around to keep an eye on Jack today." He sighed. "I really am sorry about the boat trip. And for getting you to come here for nothing."

Allegra shrugged. It was an effort to keep her feelings from showing on her face. The waste of a precious day of her holiday was galling, to say the least. But worse, the sudden change in arrangements had forced her to face the truth. She'd looked forward to spending the day in Max's company and was just as disappointed as Jack. Quickly, she turned away, averting her eyes to stare at the breathtaking view of the sea. "It's not a problem!" Obviously, he had no intention of telling her why he'd suddenly had to change his plans.

"But I'm sure you could find a more interesting way to spend the day than looking after a six-year-old."

"Perhaps. But I like Jack, and I hate to see him disappointed. Anyway, we'll both enjoy the beach."

"Thanks. I really appreciate what you're doing. I'll make it up to you. I promise."

"Oh, please!" Allegra threw him a cursory glance. "I'm doing it for Jack. Don't give it another thought."

Chapter Nine

Just as Allegra had forecast, she and Jack thoroughly enjoyed their day at the beach. They waded in the warm shallows among the tiny, darting silver fish, shrimped in the rock pools, disturbed several crabs, and played soccer on the sand—with Allegra keeping goal between two piles of pebbles.

Maria had outdone herself with the kind of picnic beloved of small boys, and Jack's appetite seemed to have perked up considerably. He was having fun, and his earlier disappointment was forgotten. Allegra focused all of her attention on him, determined not to let vengeful thoughts of Max spoil the day, and it was almost five o'clock when they gathered up their assorted belongings—which included a bucket full of shrimp—and returned to the house.

"Where's Uncle Max?" was Jack's first question.

Maria shook her head. "He has not come back yet, *querido*."

She took him to shower off the sand, and Allegra, irritated that Max hadn't shown up, went to do the same. What did he think he was playing at? What was important enough to keep him at Clearwater all this time? And exactly how long was she expected to stay here babysitting?

Maria brought them dark, delicious slices of devil's food cake and tall glasses of iced tea. Afterward they settled down to watch Jack's favorite Tom and Jerry cartoons on TV. An hour later, Jack's eyelids were beginning to droop, and Allegra touched his flushed cheek.

"Time for bed?"

The blue eyes flew open. "But I want to wait for Uncle Max!"

Allegra nodded. "He could come up and say good night to you when he gets back."

Jack shook his head. "But I might fall asleep and miss him. Sometimes, he comes home late."

I'll bet he does! Allegra thought with a piercing stab of pain and bent to pick up some of the jigsaw pieces that had fallen to the floor. *Now why does that not surprise me?* Once again, the image of Daria Cavendish on Max's arm the other evening flashed into her mind and she forced herself to smile brightly at Jack.

"Okay. You're the boss!"

But when Maria put her head around the door half an hour later, his protest was only halfhearted.

Allegra slipped a comforting arm around him. "What if I come up later to read to you?"

"Cool."

He fell asleep in the middle of one of Harry Potter's adventures, and Allegra sat for a while, looking down at the small face with the thick dark eyelashes sweeping his flushed cheeks. *I could so love this little boy,* she thought, with a sudden surge of tenderness. And immediately, she straightened the sheet over him and went downstairs before the image of another face floated into her mind.

She found Maria in the kitchen.

"Jack's fast asleep," she said. "Perhaps Carlos would be kind enough to take me back to Cedar Bay?"

Maria looked anxious. "I am sorry, Miss Howard, but Carlos, he has gone to Tampa to help his brother. He will not come home until tomorrow."

Of course! Max had mentioned that Carlos would not be around.

"And," Maria went on, "Señor Max, he has taken the powerboat."

That meant she was trapped! Virtually marooned on this island with no means of escape until Max Tempest decided to return.

"That's all right. I'll call his cell phone." Allegra forced a smile.

Her hand was trembling slightly as she dialed. When she got hold of Max, she intended to make her feelings very clear.

His phone was switched off. Typical, she thought

bleakly. There was nothing to do but wait until Mr. Tempest graciously decided to tear himself away from Clearwater and return home.

Max glanced at his watch as he went outside to use his cell phone. Eight thirty! This was the first chance he'd had to use the phone. And he probably wouldn't have bothered if he hadn't suddenly remembered that with Carlos away, Allegra was literally marooned.

"Allegra? Hi! Is everything okay?"

"How kind of you to contact me!" Allegra's voice was heavy with sarcasm.

"Hey, I'm sorry! I've been tied up all day. I've only just remembered about Carlos' trip to Tampa." He was apologetic. The business with Daria had completely taken him over.

"So what do you intend doing about it?" Her voice was icy.

There was a short silence while he debated whether to explain what was going on. Then, deciding against the idea—he had neither the time nor the inclination to go into details over the phone—he merely said, "Look, I know it's a lot to ask of you, but I'm afraid I'll have to ask you to stay put until the morning."

"Excuse me?"

"I can't leave yet, I'm needed here. It's kind of complicated. I can't explain at the moment."

He decided to take her shocked silence as a sign of acquiescence. He'd make it up to her. Anyway, he found himself thinking, it would be good to smile at her across the breakfast table in the morning. "Thanks again," he said quickly. "Just tell Maria to give you dinner and ask her to put you in a room with a view! See you tomorrow!"

'Wait!' Allegra began but he had already switched off.

The sheer nerve and the casual assumption that his wishes would be meekly obeyed had the blood pounding in Allegra's head. She stared incredulously at the receiver as she searched for the right words to express her feelings of outraged disbelief.

This man could not be serious! How could he treat her like this? Oh, yes, he'd see her tomorrow, all right—and for the last time! It would be a cold day in hell before he got the chance to take advantage of her good nature again.

She slammed the phone down and went to stand at the edge of the terrace, clutching the stone balustrade as if her life depended on it, so angry that her whole body seemed to be vibrating. It was quite obvious what he was up to! She'd been right about him all along. And if it wasn't Daria, it would be another of his victims!

The very thought of Max with another woman filled her with the kind of pain she thought she would never have to endure again. The green-eyed monster had raised its head once more, and there was nothing she could do about it. Being in love with Max tempest had never brought her anything but misery and she cursed herself for her weakness.

Maria's eyes were curious when Allegra, with set face, finally felt equal to going indoors to inform her that she would be staying the night. And what a night it was!

The beautifully appointed bedroom with its high, carved bed and exquisite furnishings was the last word in luxury and should have provided the most exacting guest with a comfortable night's sleep. French windows opened on to a balcony, and the night air, heavy with the sent of pine, drifted in. Lulled by the soft whisper of the sea on the beach below, Allegra, in a voluminous but exquisitely embroidered white cotton nightgown lent to her by Maria, slept fitfully, tossing and turning well into the early hours, and woke at eight, hot and dry-mouthed, to the sound of voices drifting up from the terrace below her window.

A quick, surreptitious glance from the balcony confirmed that the master of the house had finally returned. Coffee cup in hand, Max was deep in conversation with Maria, and by the look of him, it had obviously been quite a night. The black hair was uncombed, his chin was unshaven, and he looked pale and exhausted.

Yes, quite a night, Allegra thought savagely as she marched into the elegant marble bathroom to shower. Not that she looked a great deal better herself. She stared dispiritedly at her reflection in the mirror above the basin. The shower had revived her but had done little to refresh her heavy eyes or the bluish shadows underneath. Her face, completely bare of makeup, was pale under the newly acquired tan, and her nose had started to peel. She looked a mess, she thought. But who cared? Not Max, that was for sure. The one comfort was the discovery that Maria, bless her, must have removed her clothes at some point and returned them, washed and beautifully ironed while Allegra was still asleep. She pulled on her shorts and T-shirt, slicked back her damp hair, and secured it in a ponytail. Coffee was what she needed—buckets of the stuff. With a last, despairing look in the full-length mirror, she marched downstairs to confront Max Tempest. She intended to tell him in precise detail exactly how she felt about his behavior.

"Good morning!" He greeted her with a broad smile.

She saw that he had showered, shaved, and changed into jeans and a crisp white shirt. The mere sight of him made Allegra bristle with anger.

"Hey, thanks for all you did yesterday," he said. "I owe you one."

Ignoring the comment, she flounced into the chair opposite as Maria appeared at her side like a genie, wielding a vast silver coffeepot.

"Thank you so much for laundering my things," Allegra said to her.

"A pleasure." Maria beamed. "You would like some breakfast?"

"Just coffee, thanks." Allegra spooned sugar vengefully into her cup and added cream. Normally she drank her coffee black and sugarless, but today she needed comfort.

"Sleep okay?" Max asked with grave courtesy. There was amusement somewhere behind the polite expression.

"Thanks to you, I hardly slept at all," Allegra snapped, reddening.

Max raised his eyebrows quizzically. "Thanks to me? Should I be flattered?"

That was it. The final straw. She knew, by the sudden light-headed feeling of rage, that she was about to lose it. She heard the provoking note in his voice and exploded.

"Flattered? You must be joking! I couldn't sleep because I was furious. I couldn't believe that anyone could treat a so-called guest so disrespectfully."

"I take it you're referring to yesterday's fiasco?"

"Of course I mean that! I was literally marooned here!"

Max had the grace to look shamefaced. "I realized I was imposing on you, but when I called and asked you to stay, you didn't object."

"You didn't give me the chance!" Allegra raged. "You hung up on me!"

The expression in his eyes hardened. "Hardly. I was in a hurry."

"Oh, please!"

Stung by her tone, Max's eyes hardened. "As I was about to explain, Daria Cavendish needed my help yesterday."

"Really?" Allegra snapped. "Well, lucky old Daria! What a shame you couldn't show the same interest in your nephew's welfare!"

Max's mouth set in a hard line. "I knew he was in safe hands."

"Excuse me! I'm not a professional childminder!"

"I'm aware of that." He shrugged. "But you offered to help, and I thought you were a friend I could rely on, that's all."

"So you could spend time with your latest girlfriend?"

"What?" Max stared at her, his eyes like molten steel. "Daria? My latest girlfriend? Are you out of your mind?"

"Far from it! Oh, come on, Max. It's common knowledge!" Allegra met his eyes bravely enough, but the look of utter contempt on Max's face robbed her voice of conviction.

"You can't be serious!" He shook his head in disbelief. "Daria Cavendish is eighteen years old. She also happens to be my goddaughter. She needed me yesterday because she'd got herself into a spot of trouble." He smiled contemptuously at the horrified expression on Allegra's face. "Satisfied?"

Suddenly, she was floundering. "Trouble? But you said . . . I thought . . ."

"I know what you thought," Max snapped. "And you got it wrong! Would you believe that sitting all day and most of the night by a hospital bed is not exactly my idea of fun?"

There was a silence as they eyed each other, one with cold dislike, the other with disbelief.

"Hospital?" Allegra's voice was suddenly less emphatic. "Daria—in hospital? Why?"

"It's got nothing to do with you." He got to his feet and glanced at his watch. "Carlos is on his way back. In fact, he should be here soon. He can take you back to your hotel whenever you're ready."

Allegra, with the wind suddenly taken out of her sails, went on staring at him.

"You could have told me last night. Why the big secret?"

"And have you dashing off one of your slick little pieces to your editor? Forget it!" His mouth twisted. "Good-bye, Allegra. Enjoy the rest of your vacation." He spun on his heel and strode across the terrace.

Allegra clenched her hands in impotent fury as she stared at his retreating back. How dare he speak to her like that! To imply that she was some kind of unscrupulous newshound, out to ruin an innocent girl's reputation? All right, she'd been a little crazy to have imagined that Max would have had her babysitting while he romanced Daria. If she hadn't spent the entire evening winding herself up with jealous thoughts, she would probably have realized he would never have been so obvious.

She groaned as he disappeared down the steps to the beach, and her cheeks flamed as she remembered the accusations she'd flung at him. She'd been so determined to remain detached and icy-calm—to deliver her carefully rehearsed lines with clinical precision before making a dignified exit. Instead, she'd lost it completely!

But why blame herself? Max was so determined to keep up with this cloak-and-dagger nonsense, and as a result she was continually left to draw her own conclusions. Why couldn't he have leveled with her from the start?

"Hey!" She turned as Jack, scrubbed and pink-cheeked from his morning tub, appeared at her side.

The last vestiges of her anger melted as she looked at him. "Good morning!"

"Where's Uncle Max?" he asked. "Did he eat breakfast yet?"

"He went to the beach, I think." Allegra forced a smile.

The boy's face brightened. "I'll go see him."

As he ran across the terrace, Maria appeared with Max's breakfast and looked at her, puzzled.

"I've sent Jack to find his uncle," Allegra muttered, embarrassed.

Maria sighed. "Señor Max, he should eat. He is exhausted." She shook her head. "He has not slept all night."

Allegra bit her lip. "So I understand."

"He worry too much. Is too kind." Maria added darkly as she went indoors, "Miss Daria, she is trouble. Always wanting him to help."

People kept telling her that Max was kind, Allegra thought grimly. It would be really nice to be on the receiving end sometime!

She went to stand at the edge of the terrace to look out over the bay, hoping to catch a glimpse of Carlos returning. Suddenly, she remembered what he had told her about Max helping out his brother's family. Annoying as he was, the man had some redeeming features and the people who worked for him clearly adored him.

She turned away from the empty sea with a sigh, pacing up and down the terrace in a frenzy of impatience. Trapped again, she thought angrily. And all because she had been unable to say no to temptation and stay away from Max Tempest once her work was finished. If she hadn't weakly agreed to the sailing trip, she would now be as free as a bird, blamelessly enjoying what was left of her vacation.

She clenched her fists in the pockets of her shorts and gave a groan of self-disgust. Much as she hated to admit it, in seven years, nothing had really changed.

She was still as helpless, still as unable to resist Max, as she had been at seventeen. She felt the same attraction, the same hopeless fascination she had known all that time ago. And worse, the mere thought of his involvement with another woman filled her with the same desperate jealousy.

She had to admit she had been quick to judge Max. Had been too willing to listen to gossip, too quick to believe what she had read about his reputation. But from the very first moment, he had set out to be deliberately evasive. Surely, he had known her well enough to trust her and if not, she wanted suddenly to know the reason why.

"We caught twenty-two shrimps and we found a cave and I scored eight goals." Jack's boyish treble carried quite clearly from where he and Max sat on the fallen trunk of a palm tree, skimming pebbles across the surface of the water. Neither had noticed the unwilling eavesdropper standing at the bottom of the steps a few yards behind them . . .

"Allegra's a great player, though," Jack added loyally. "For a girl."

"I'll bet she is." Max's voice was dry, tinged with faint amusement. Then he turned his head and looked over his shoulder and met her eyes.

"Allegra!" Jack smiled at her. "Want to try skimming? I'll find you some flat pebbles, if you like." He jumped off his perch and began to search among the rocks.

Allegra picked her way over the rocks and joined Max. "I couldn't leave until I'd spoken to you," she said. "There are one or two things I want to say before I go."

Max brought his arm back and sent another pebble bouncing across the water. "Be my guest."

"I think it's a pity you hadn't been honest with me from the start."

Max frowned. "About?"

"Everything. It was obvious to me right away that you really didn't want to do the interview."

"True."

"So, why waste my time? And, incidentally, your own?"

"It wasn't personal. It was just not something I wanted to do at this particular time. I came here because I needed space. I wanted to spend some private time with Jack, make decisions about the future."

"I can understand that. Still . . ."

"My agent leaned on me," Max broke in. "As simple as that."

She shrugged. "I suppose you could say my editor did the same to me. I didn't want this assignment any more than you did. When I knew it was you, I felt like running a mile. Perhaps I should have."

"I'm glad you didn't." His voice had softened, and he turned to face her, his eyes asking her to forgive him. "I'm sorry about yesterday."

"Would it have been so hard to tell me about Daria?"

"You never asked." Max grinned at the outraged expression on her face. "Listen—about the way I behaved—it was selfish of me to let you give up your whole day. And then to expect you to stay put overnight—I guess you had every right to be mad at me! Do you think we might start over again? Let bygones be bygones?"

"What are bygones?" Jack, returning with his hands full of pebbles, looked inquiringly from one to the other, and his uncle put out a hand and brushed the hair out of his eyes.

"Things that don't matter," Max said. He stood up and grinned at Allegra. "You'd better start making use of all these stones."

Allegra shook her head, laughing. "I'm no good at it, I'm afraid." She proceeded to demonstrate the fact, as pebble after pebble sank without trace, despite Jack's sympathetic yells of encouragement.

"Let me show you."

Max reached out and drew her toward him, standing close behind her as he showed her how to hold the stone. Held in the circle of his arm, the soft warmth of her made him catch her breath. "It's all in the wrist action," he said, cupping her elbow as he brought her arm gently back.

"Like this?"

He didn't want to throw stones. He wanted to turn and brush her mouth with his, wanted to hold her closer until he saw her eyes soften and then blaze with the same longing that was suddenly consuming him. As if she was feeling the same sensation, she suddenly jerked her arm out of his grasp and flung the pebble as hard as she could. It hit the surface of the sea and bounced twice before sinking with a small splash.

"All right!" Jack punched the air in excitement. "Throw another one!"

Allegra laughed. "To quote one of my dad's favorite sayings, I think I'll quit while I'm ahead."

Max looked from one to the other—at Allegra's laughing face, at Jack's eager one, and suddenly, he wanted to clasp them both in his arms and never let them go.

Instead, he turned away and brushed the sand from his fingers. "Jack, why don't you run on up to the house and use your charm on Maria? Allegra and I could use some coffee."

They watched in silence as he ran toward the steps. Now that they were alone, there was a sudden constraint between them, and Allegra wasn't sure how to deal with it.

"Is Daria seriously ill?" she asked. "I promise you I have no ulterior motives in asking, whatever you may think. There'll be no slick little article, as you put it."

"That was a cheap shot, I must admit." Max had the grace to look ashamed. "Daria's going to be okay—this time. But the kid has problems. She's been working in Miami this summer, and I haven't much liked what I've seen. She has too much money. And I guess success came too early. She's a good kid at heart, but she mixes with the wrong crowd."

Max tossed one last pebble into the sea, and the ripples spread out over the surface of the milky water.

"Her parents split up when she was Jack's age," he went on. "Her father spoiled her, and when he died last year, she took it hard." He sighed. "Hugh and I were good buddies, and I've always tried to look out for her. But it's easier said than done."

Allegra nodded. "Not easy."

"Yesterday," Max continued grimly, "She ended up in the hospital, full of booze and pills after a wild party. A real little chemical plant, the doctor called her." He shook his head. "They told me she was out of the woods when I got there. But later on, she took a turn for the worse. She suddenly stopped breathing, and it was touch and go for a time. I had to make certain she would be okay before I left."

"If I'd known that. . . ." Allegra's cheeks colored.

"She'll be fine," he said. "Maybe she's learned her lesson. Anyhow, I got in touch with her mother She's going to try and get out here to spend some time with her.

"I should have explained, but I didn't want to go into all the details last night. And anyway, it's become second nature to keep my mouth shut. I'm sorry, it's just my way of keeping a low profile."

"You could have trusted me, you know."

"I do. Why would I invite you to my home? Ask you to take care of my nephew?" He reached for her, his hands gently drawing her close. "I think," he said quietly, "it might just be the other way around, don't you? Maybe it's time you started trusting me."

He lifted a strand of sun-bleached hair that had escaped her ponytail and wound it around his fingers. Then his hand cupped her chin as his mouth claimed hers, softly at first and then, as she responded helplessly to his kiss, hungrily, parting her lips with exquisite sweetness as he pressed her against him.

Then he released her, watching her face.

"At least," he said, rather unsteadily, "give it some thought."

Dazed and confused, her lips tingling from his kiss, she was suddenly bereft of words.

"Have dinner with me tonight." It was not so much an invitation as a command. "We could get out of town. Drive south a little ways." He took her hand to lead her up the crumbling steps. "I guess you and I have quite a lot to talk about."

Chapter Ten

Allegra stood on the sidewalk just outside the hotel waiting for Max to arrive. She felt a strange heady sensation of anticipation, a melting away of the antagonism the thought of him often aroused in her when she was alone. There was a sense of danger too, the kind of delicious frisson of fear she'd felt as a child, queuing to ride the roller coaster at the local fair.

What on earth, she asked herself, did she think she was playing at? One kiss, some soft, persuasive words, had been all it took to break down all her carefully constructed barriers. And here she stood like a schoolgirl on her first date, tingling with excitement and hoping. . . . *Don't even go there,* she told herself. If ever there was a recipe for disaster, that was it.

The street was crawling with tourists, and she tried not to imagine that those who passed by were staring at her curiously. This is what it must be like to conduct an illicit affair, she thought with a certain grim amusement as she glanced nervously over her shoulder, half expecting to see a gang of paparazzi sneaking into view.

For heaven's sake! So what if she was seen getting into Max Tempest's car? All she was doing was meeting an old friend. And who would be remotely interested in her, anyway? Max might make good copy—but she certainly wouldn't!

Even so, knowing Max's antipathy to the press, she very much hoped, as the seconds crawled by, that there was no one around to stir up trouble.

Max felt tense. Wired. He was not used to feeling anxious before a date. It never mattered to him what the occasion was. He was used to being in control of the situation, and his dates were only too happy to spend time in his company.

The thing was, he wasn't at all sure that Allegra would be there waiting for him. This morning she'd been furious. And he didn't blame her. There had been no need to keep her in the dark about Daria's latest scrape. But he had acquired his mistrust of the press the hard way. It had become an automatic reaction—a habit he couldn't easily shake and absolutely nothing to do with the way he felt about Allegra. In a way, it was a relief to admit to himself the unassailable fact that he'd fallen for her all over again—this time, with all the maturity and experience of his thirty-seven years.

The problem was that he wasn't sure he could offer her the kind of life she deserved. She might not be willing to share his love with another woman's child.

Maybe she wouldn't settle for anything less than his entire heart. And if that was the case, it was hopeless even to think of any kind of future with her.

Despite his misgivings, she was there waiting for him as he drew up outside the hotel—and at the sight of her, his spirits lifted.

She must have guessed he was anxious to make a quick, discreet getaway and made sure she was there early enough to guarantee that happened. Another woman might have been disappointed by the sight of Carlos' battered old Chevy, would have preferred to draw attention to herself by stepping into the kind of car that proclaimed Max's film-star status. But not Allegra. She would have hated that sort of notoriety— would have moved heaven and earth to avoid it.

She was smiling, her eyes dancing at the sight of him behind the wheel as he leaned across to push the door open for her. She slid into the passenger seat beside him, calm and clearly unfazed by the way he gunned the old engine to life and roared off down the street.

"I hope you're not a nervous passenger!" he said with a sideways grin.

"That rather depends on the driver." She looked at him and laughed, and suddenly he felt liberated—free of the shackles of the life he had been living for so many years. There was nowhere he would rather be at that moment than cruising down the Florida highway in an old jalopy with Allegra at his side. Some things were far more important than money, success, and one's name in lights.

He leaned over to switch on the radio and as he did

so caught the scent of her perfume—and managed in that brief movement to notice everything about her. The slim brown legs stretched out in front of her, her small beautiful hands lying in her lap, the gentle curves beneath the jade-green sundress she was wearing, the gold of her hair twisted into a topknot on the crown of her head.

"I feel about seventeen," he said softly, "sneaking my dad's car to take my girl out for a ride."

He reached for her hand, lifted it to his lips, went on holding it as he drove the car down the freeway.

If he hadn't been concentrating on the road ahead, he might have seen her quick, shy sideways glance.

"Where are we going?" She sounded a little breathless.

"There's a place I'd like you to see, off the beaten track. Just a beach I know where we can walk and watch the sun set."

He glanced at her, trying to gauge her reaction. But her eyes were fixed on the sparkling waters of the Gulf of Mexico, entranced by the vista unfolding before them.

Max turned the car off the road and down a narrow track between mangrove and pines. And then, before them, between the palms and the water, the beach curved, sickle-shaped, and Allegra caught her breath.

Max switched off the engine, turning to her. "It's quite a view," he said softly, "but I'd rather look at you."

He drew her toward him, and her mouth was warm and eager against his.

"Tell me you're glad you came," he said softly.

"Very glad."

He kissed her again, his mouth gentle on her lips, and he felt her tremble at his touch. The scent of her, the feel of her in his arms, released all those buried memories. As she gave herself up to the rapture of his kiss, he felt the last vestiges of her resistance melt away, she slid her arms around his neck, and he knew that this was what he had been longing for ever since she'd walked back into his life.

He raised his head and looked down into her face, saw in her eyes the same look of sweet surrender that he remembered from all those years ago.

He wanted to tell her what was in his heart, but suddenly he had no idea what to say or where to start. So, he thought self-mockingly, Max the so-called lady-killer was tongue-tied. And as he racked his brain for the right words, she slipped out of his arms, gently released him, and turned to fumble with the door.

Allegra swung her feet out onto the fine, sugary sand. "Just a second." She took his outstretched hand, leaning against Max for a moment as she slipped off her shoes. Smiling, he took them from her and tossed them into the backseat.

"It's not too far."

And then, as if it was the most natural thing in the world, he took her hand in his as they walked along the beach.

The sand was surprisingly cold under her bare feet. They walked slowly, her hand curled in his firm clasp, and Allegra felt a sudden surge of happiness. Fragments of their conversation came back to her. "My girl." That is what he had said. "Seventeen again . . . taking my girl for a ride."

Her breath caught in her throat. If only it was that simple. If only they could wipe out seven years, go back and start again. No! She couldn't even begin to think like this! She had to focus on something ordinary—practical.

"I forgot to bring your jacket! I'm sorry. I have a memory like a sieve."

He laughed. "I think I can just about manage without it tonight."

"You could come up to get it later." She blushed deeply, afraid he might think that was an invitation. "Or," she rushed on desperately, "wait in the car while I run in to fetch it."

"What?" he said, his mouth twitching at her obvious confusion. "And risk becoming prey to any passing paparazzi?"

She laughed. "As if anyone would expect you, of all people, to emerge from that car!"

"You'd be surprised! Tomorrow morning, you may well find yourself on the front page of the tabloids." He grinned. "I can see the headlines now. 'Mystery Blond Snatched by Deranged Actor.'"

Her reserve crumbled. "It would make good copy," she said, laughing. "I was pretty nervous standing there waiting. I didn't realize it was you at first. You must admit, that car doesn't quite go with the image."

"It actually belongs to Carlos. He lets me borrow it now and again—when I need to be particularly discreet."

Allegra raised an eyebrow. No need to wonder why. Obviously, she wasn't the first to be collected in the disreputable old jalopy.

"I don't quite know how," Max said, "but I seem to have an uncanny ability to read your mind. If you're thinking that I use the Chevy as a kind of love wagon, you couldn't be more wrong. The last time I borrowed it was to take Jack out for the day."

Oops! She'd put her foot in it again. Believing the worst of him. Expecting him to behave like the love rat dreamed up by the tabloids—when in fairness, she'd found no evidence to support any of their wild theories.

"This image of mine," he said, "it's a myth. I'd like you to believe that." He grinned bleakly. "I've lost count of the number of women I'm supposed to have cast aside!"

There had been so many stories about Max, some of them pretty colorful.

"It got so bad a couple of years back that I couldn't risk being seen in public with any woman. Which is why I've gone to such lengths to make sure we have a little privacy tonight. Believe me, if I'd been crazy enough to take you to dinner, the press would have had a field day. It wouldn't take them long to start on you. Before you knew it, they'd have been digging up all the details they could find about your background."

Allegra smiled. "Nothing very sensational there, I'm afraid."

"They wouldn't find that a problem. Their powers of invention are phenomenal! A few years back, I was crazy enough to invite an attractive woman I met at a party out to dinner. The next thing I knew, she'd sold her story to some lurid magazine, giving a totally fictitious account of the evening—which, I may tell you, included some pretty inventive details." He shrugged. "There was nothing I could do about it without attracting even more adverse publicity."

"It must be tough."

"As you once reminded me, it goes with the territory. And I shouldn't complain. The movie industry has been good to me. I just want you to understand where that paranoia of mine comes from. And now it's even more important for me to keep a low profile."

"Yes?" She glanced up at the note of seriousness in his voice.

"But that'll keep." He pointed toward the end of the beach, where she saw a ramshackle wooden building backed by leaning pines. "Let's eat."

She raised an eyebrow. "That's a restaurant?"

He grinned at her puzzled, faintly wary expression. "Wait and see."

They walked toward what appeared to be a tumble-down shack with a rickety veranda running the length of it and the name "Gino's Bar and Grill" painted in un-even white letters above the porch. It was apparently deserted, apart from the large, smiling bartender who greeted Max like a long-lost friend and shook Allegra's hand with grave courtesy. It was the last place on earth Allegra would have expected to find a movie star. That was, until she had sampled the bill of fare.

"There's no menu," Max explained. "It's either alli-gator tails, catfish, or sardines probably caught a few hours ago. I'd recommend the latter—they're the best in town."

Allegra smiled. Alligator? Catfish? Sardines? No contest! "I think I'll take your advice."

Everything about that evening was memorable. The food, eaten with their fingers, straight from the barbecue and served with crusty Cuban bread. The view, indigo sea and red-gold sunset. Allegra tried to commit every detail to memory. A night like this could never happen again.

"When do they expect you back in London?" he asked her.

"I'm due back in work next Monday."

"That gives us five days."

Us? She tried to ignore the little frisson of excitement the word evoked in her. Just a slip of the tongue. No big deal! But she couldn't finish the piece of key lime pie, delicious as it was.

Gino brought them thimble-size cups of very sweet, very black café cubano. Max laughed at her shocked expression as she took her first sip.

"I should have warned you. The stuff is strong enough to make your hair stand on end."

"It'll probably keep me awake half the night." She smiled ruefully. It wouldn't just be the coffee preventing her from sleeping! "I had no idea places like this existed. How on earth do they keep going? We seem to be the only customers!"

"They do most of their trade during the day and early evening. It's mostly local because there are no amenities and it's off the main drag. It's a place I can bring Jack and feel fairly certain of being left in peace."

She glanced across at him. In the semidarkness, it was impossible to read his expression. She wanted to ask questions—dozens of them—but restrained herself, not wanting anything to destroy the ambience of their evening.

Max saved her the trouble.

"I think maybe it's time I came clean about my plans for him," he said. "I'm hoping to get custody. Eventually, to legally adopt him. Maybe you guessed?"

If it had fleetingly crossed her mind, she had dismissed the thought as highly unlikely. With Max's lifestyle, how could he give enough time and attention to bringing up a child? He himself had admitted he had no experience of dealing with children and found dealing with Jack daunting at times. And in any case, it might be difficult for any single man to adopt a child.

"I expect you find the idea as crazy as I do," Max said. "I know so little about kids, and most of the time I'm scared Jack can see right through me."

"He really means a lot to you, doesn't he?" Allegra said.

"I had no idea how much until I got to know him. Okay, it won't be easy, but I'll give it my best shot."

"The other day, when I found him at the marina, he told me how much he misses his mother. How she'd want him to be with you. And how he'd like that."

"I know he wants to stay with me." Max nodded. "The poor kid's been passed around like a parcel. But I really don't want to get his hopes up. Not yet, anyway."

He took out his billfold and tucked what seemed to

Allegra to be a ridiculously large number of dollar bills under his plate. "Let's walk."

The mood had changed. The easy camaraderie between them as they ate their meal had become something quite different. She sensed in him a need to talk, to share something of himself with her. He didn't just take her hand as before. Instead, he drew it under his arm, pressing it against his side in a gesture of intimacy that filled her with strange tenderness.

They walked slowly across the dark, deserted beach, and the night enfolded them, the air sultry and sweet, heavy with the scent of pine.

"Tell me about Jack's mother." She sensed that he wanted her to ask him. He was not a man who found it easy to unburden himself, and he needed her prompting.

"She was five years younger than me. A great kid. We were pretty close. She was only fifteen when my parents were killed in an automobile wreck. I guess she kind of went off the rails for a while." His voice was expressionless, but Allegra sensed the emotion beneath the surface.

"She was beautiful," he said, "and talented. Got into modeling straight after high school and looked as if she was going to make a name for herself. I thought she was doing okay, but then things started to go wrong. She got in with the wrong crowd. The usual scenario. Drugs. Drinking. I didn't know how to handle it, and I blame myself for not trying harder. I should have been there for her—looked out for her. But at the time, I was really into myself. My career came first. I guess I was pretty selfish." He shook his head. "Why do you think I'm so keen to help Daria? I don't want to mess up a second time. I'd never forgive myself."

Of course. Allegra blushed in the darkness as she remembered the tantrum she'd pulled when he'd returned yesterday.

"When I found out my kid sister was pregnant," Max went on, "it was a wake-up call. I realized how self-centered I'd been, and I tried to make up for the way I'd treated her. The guy responsible wouldn't have wanted to know, and she never told him. In fact, she never told me or anyone else his name. So I took her home and made her move in with me until Jack was born."

"So you were part of Jack's life from the beginning."

"For a while. I hadn't seen her so happy for a long time. Having Jack seemed to turn her life around. I found her a small apartment, and she went back to school after Jack was old enough to go to kindergarten. She even started dating again, and then she got sick. She should have got herself checked out right away, but she left it until it was too late."

They were almost at the water's edge, and the tiny wavelets were sparkling with phosphorescence.

"You almost met her!" Max said. "That last night. At that party in London?"

Allegra's heart clutched. "At Julia's party?"

"Yes." He gave a rueful grin. "It was really bad timing. We were arguing, remember?"

How could she ever forget? She stopped, staring up at him. "You mean that attractive, dark-haired girl was your sister?"

She looked up at him, stricken. The girl's face had haunted her for so long!

"Yes," he said. "That was Annie. She'd been living in Paris for the past year, and she'd come to London, looking for me. If she hadn't arrived when she did, it might all have been a very different story. I'd met a girl, you see. At a backstage party. I'd fallen for her. Big time." He stopped walking and turned her gently toward him, laying his hand on her cheek. "Don't tell me you didn't know."

Of course she hadn't known! How could she have known when he had treated her like some starstruck groupie and sent her packing?

"I don't think I wanted to admit how I felt—even to myself," he said, reading the bewildered expression on her face. "Then Annie arrived out of the blue, and you disappeared."

She looked up at him with wondering eyes. "But I thought . . ."

He put a gentle finger over her mouth. "You haven't heard the whole sad story yet."

Annie's sudden arrival that night had changed everything.

"There was my kid sister, alone in the world, far from home and pregnant. She needed me. I thought about calling you to explain, but then I figured it was best left alone. Annie had been abandoned by this older guy, and somehow that had echoes. When you turned up that night on my doorstep, she was there. I let you believe I was with someone else."

"But why?" Allegra asked, trying to fathom the expression on his face. "You must have realized how I felt."

"I was leaving the following week for the States to make my first film. There was Annie—I had to take care of her. I was going to have my hands full for a while. And there was the gap in our ages. You were working your way through school." He shrugged. "I honestly believed you'd be better off if I got out of your life before things got even more complicated."

Perhaps, she thought, he had been right. She had been very young. Too young to deal with the challenges life had thrown Max at that particular time. But not anymore!

"And now?" she asked, looking up into his face.

"Now, more complications. There's Jack, and I want to make sure he has a secure upbringing. I know it's not going to be easy, but I have to give it my best shot."

"Of course," she said and heard her voice catch in her throat.

"Another thing. I've done quite a lot of soul-searching lately, and I've made my final decision. No more films. It really won't be a sacrifice. I know now that my career isn't the most important thing in my life." He threw her a sideways glance. "It's kind of liberating, knowing that."

"I suppose it must be. Though I can't imagine ever wanting to give up my writing."

"Well, like I say, my work no longer means that much to me. I'm a country boy at heart. I have a place in Wyoming where it would be perfect for Jack to grow up."

"You really mean that?" Allegra couldn't disguise her surprise.

"Sure. I've had my fill of running around the world. I've had a great time, but acting doesn't excite me anymore. Anyway, back there in those mountains, I'd have the time to devote to Jack. I know I'm doing the right thing. Jack needs stability in his life, a loving home. And I can provide it." He paused. "I figure the only thing missing would be a wife."

Allegra's mouth dried up. Dear Lord! A wife! She looked away quickly in case he could see her heart in her eyes. Was that just a flippant, throwaway remark? She felt suddenly short of breath, and her heart seemed to be doing cartwheels inside her chest. It was crazy stuff—the words of a desperate man determined to get his way, whatever the cost. He would do anything, she thought, to improve his chances of adopting Jack. Oh Lord! If only. . . . It would be so easy to be a stepmother to a child like Jack. So easy to love him—to love them both—to be part of their lives.

And then he turned to look at her.

All evening she had managed somehow to keep her emotions in check, had listened calmly as he opened his heart to her.

For a long, tremulous moment, their eyes locked and held. And then the fragile shell of Allegra's self-control shattered and she reached for him, her arms holding him close as they sank, still clinging to each other to the soft, yielding sand.

She lifted a hand to touch his face, and as she did so, he took it and pressed his mouth to her open palm. And with his touch, the world began to spin.

Trembling, she ran her fingers across his face, and she saw him close his eyes, heard the sharp intake of breath as she traced the contours of his mouth, softly at first and then with sudden, urgent pressure. He bent his head, and when he kissed her, a wave of pure sensation broke over her and set her on fire.

Max was lost. The touch of Allegra's lips had robbed him of the self-control he had always prided himself on. It was as if she had taken away some strong, vital part of him and rendered him helpless. He raised his head, dragging his lips from her sweet warm mouth, feeling her soft breath on his cheek.

He had closed his eyes, afraid he might see in her face some element of doubt or even reluctance. But when he looked at her at last, he saw only a longing that matched his.

He reached for her and found her mouth again, felt her tremble as he cradled her head in his hands. For a split second, he thought that the bright flashes that seemed to light up the entire beach were in his head.

And then as Allegra went rigid in his arms, he lifted his head, the dark figure wielding the camera making off across the sand with lightning speed.

Cursing, Max struggled to his feet and began to give chase, his feet sinking in the soft sand. He knew there was little hope of catching up—the guy must have had fifteen yards on him—but he persisted, his breath rasping in his throat as he raced across the beach, his mind empty of everything except his need to get his hands on the photographer.

He had reached the spot where he had left his car when he saw the frantic figure hurl himself into the convertible parked a few yards behind the Chevy. A wrench of the wheel, a screech of tires as the car was thrown into reverse, and it was gone, its taillights flashing an insolent signal of triumph as it disappeared down the track.

He'd lost him! But not before he'd recognized the shock of white-blond hair and the impudent grin. Rick Fielding. Of course—who else? And at that moment, Max had felt as agonized and as winded as if someone had kicked him hard in the stomach. Tonight, he would have trusted Allegra with his life. And as he turned and saw the slim figure hurrying across the beach toward him, he could almost taste the bitterness of her betrayal in his mouth.

"He got away!" Allegra slowed to walk the last few steps, breathing hard, her calf muscles aching from the trek through the sand. "Oh, Max! What a shame! I thought you'd manage to catch him up!"

She reached out to touch him and then drew back as she saw the furious expression on his face.

"Did you?" The voice was ice-cold as he turned and led the way to the car. "Believe me, if I had, you'd have known all about it."

For a second or two, she didn't move, struck by the harshness of his response. How could it be her fault that he'd been stalked by one of the ever-present paparazzi? She hadn't asked to be brought here. It hadn't been her idea to spend the evening together. And if they'd been photographed in rather intimate circumstances—well, it took two to tango!

She frowned. Whatever had happened between them in the past, she had honestly believed that tonight had been the beginning of something real. She hadn't imagined the depth of feeling back there on the beach. Or had she? Carried away by her own feelings, she might easily have mistaken his ardor for something else.

She got into the car beside him, keeping carefully to her side, feeling utterly insignificant. And as they began the drive back to Cedar Bay, her heart, which had been so full of hope a few minutes ago, was leaden with disappointment. Perhaps, after all, the arrival of the photographer had been a timely intervention. It had at least saved her from making a fool of herself all over again. But as she sat there beside him, the thought was far from comforting.

Max felt sick at heart. Empty. He had believed himself impervious to the kind of pain he was presently experiencing. He had always been able to walk away unscathed when it came to relationships. Apart from that one time, which he'd tried to put behind him. It was obviously a case of history repeating itself. It had been Allegra who had gotten to him seven years ago. And now here he was again! Full of angst and feeling the same sense of disillusionment that he had felt all that time ago in London.

Why had he let it happen? Why hadn't he seen it coming? Tonight, when he'd picked her up, she'd seemed so relaxed and happy to be in his company. That simple little meal, followed by the slow walk along the beach, had been as near to perfection as a romantic evening could get. Surely, he hadn't imagined the sympathy and understanding of her response as he'd confided in her?

She was obviously in the wrong profession, he thought bitterly. She should have been an actress. Her timing had been faultless.

He was so angry that he could not bring himself to glance at her as she sat there at his side in silence. Oh, she was clever. Saying nothing to implicate herself, quite confident that he hadn't recognized Fielding in the darkness. As far as she was concerned, the set-up had been perfect. She must have let her accomplice know where and when she'd be picked up. And the rest had been easy. He should have trusted his instincts that night in the restaurant. As soon as he'd lain eyes on the guy, he'd sensed there was something phony about him. They'd looked pretty cozy, the two of them. He remembered the look on Allegra's face when she'd glanced up and seen him standing there with Daria. What was it? Embarrassment? Guilt?

She hadn't even flinched when he'd told her earlier that evening about the first time he'd been set up. But she must have been amused as she watched him fall for the same kind of con all over again!

As his knuckles tightened on the wheel, she suddenly broke the silence. "Perhaps," she said hesitantly, "it won't be as bad as you think. It was . . ."—she paused—"only a kiss . . ."

He gave a short angry laugh. That was all it had meant to her! And he had imagined she felt as he did! "You're right!" he snarled. "The guy must have been disappointed! It could have been so much juicier!"

The harsh words were intended to hurt, and he knew without even looking at her that they had hit the mark.

"Max! You're driving too fast!" The sudden touch of her fingers on his arm was like fire on his skin, and as he eased his foot off the throttle, he knew why he was so angry. It wasn't just the fact that he'd been photographed. Or the knowledge that Allegra had been prepared to sell him down the river for the sake of her job. It was because he had known down there on that moonlit beach that he wanted Allegra Howard more than he had ever wanted any other woman. Wanted her in his arms. Wanted to offer her his heart. Wanted to share his life with her. For a brief moment he'd thought he'd found what he'd always been searching for. He'd been wrong, and the disappointment he felt overwhelmed him.

Chapter Eleven

"**I**'m certain no one would bother printing a photo like that."

They had almost reached the hotel after what seemed like an interminable journey. The silence between them was palpable, and Allegra was desperate to break it.

He tossed her a contemptuous glance. "Yeah, right."

"Oh, Max!" Suddenly, she lost patience. "For heaven's sake! He couldn't have gotten a decent shot of our faces! We could have been anybody."

Max's mouth twisted. "If that's supposed to make me feel better, forget it."

"I'm just trying to . . ."

"Forget it, Allegra. You're missing the point! The guy was there. Taking the photograph." He turned the car into the forecourt of the Cedar Bay and pulled up with a jerk. "You've had your pound of flesh. I had no idea until tonight that you felt you needed to get your own back. Well, you made it, and I hope it makes you happy."

"What?" Allegra stared at him, struggling to make sense of what he was saying. What on earth was he talking about? And why was he looking at her so accusingly with eyes like molten steel?

"I don't suppose it matters much to you—but can you imagine how a shot like plastered all over the papers might affect my chances of getting custody?"

Allegra recoiled at his words. No wonder he was so angry. But, dear Lord, it really wasn't her fault! It hadn't been her idea to go walking on the beach in the first place!

He leaned across her to free the door catch, his right arm brushing hers. It was unintentional, but even so, her breath caught in her throat.

"You'll forgive me if I don't get out." He straightened up and gave a brief semblance of a smile. "Oh, and by the way, you can tell Fielding that his timing was just a fraction off. A few more seconds and who knows?"

Half out of the car, she turned, her eyes narrowing as she struggled to make sense of his words. Then, her eyes widening, "Did you say Fielding?"

Max gave a savage grin. "You actually thought I didn't see the guy? I recognized him, all right! Saw him quite clearly. Just before he made off."

"It was Rick? Are you sure?" She stared at his angry face incredulously.

"Oh, come on, Allegra. I told no one I was seeing you tonight. Or where I was going. You were the only one who could possibly have tipped Rick Fielding off. I just hope you're proud of yourself."

He left her standing there in utter disbelief, staring after him as he roared off down the street.

Allegra was in shock as she walked, zombielike, across the foyer. Was it true? Was it really Rick who had sneaked up on them on the beach? But if so, what did he think he was playing at? He was a respected freelance photographer, not some lowlife hack on the make. And in any case, how could he have possibly known that she and Max were together?

"Are you all right, Miss Howard?" The friendly reception manager walking toward her was clearly struck by her pallor and the dazed expression on her face.

"What? Oh, yes, thanks. Just some bad news," she muttered, hurrying past him into the elevator. By the time she reached her room, she was still struggling with a whole catalog of emotions from disbelief to righteous anger. Max really believed she had set him up! How could he have imagined she could do such a thing? Did he honestly think she would ever have behaved with such contemptible cynicism even if she'd wanted, as he clearly believed, some kind of revenge? Did he actually see her as an immoral little gold digger, willing to sell her sordid little story to the highest bidder?

She closed the door behind her, leaning against it for a few moments. What sort of opinion did Max have of her? Surely he knew how she felt about him? How could he not have known that her passionate response to him tonight had been anything other than genuine?

As for Rick—his behavior was beneath contempt.

She'd never totally trusted him—but even so, she couldn't believe he'd stoop so low. How had he known they'd be there on that beach? He must have seen her get into the car and decided to follow them!

A soft tap on the door sent the adrenaline rushing through her veins. Max! He'd come to apologize . . . to explain. Her hands shook as she wrenched open the door.

"Room service, ma'am." The waiter, holding a tray with a jug of what looked like hot chocolate, smiled at her. "With the compliments of the management."

Desperately disappointed, Allegra forced a smile, murmured her thanks, and took the tray, closing the door hastily before the tears threatening to spill over betrayed her. She took a deep breath as she put the tray down carefully on the table. *Don't cry,* she ordered herself fiercely. But in the end, it wasn't the thought of Max Tempest but the simple act of kindness from a stranger that sent her over the edge. And she sat with her face in her hands and cried her heart out.

Max stared out of his study window into the darkness. There was an unbearable ache in his throat at the thought of the way Allegra had so callously set him up, the woman who had lain in his arms, with her eyes and lips promising him the world, who had made him feel that he was as precious to her as life itself. He had trusted her completely, and now he saw that every word she had uttered, every look, every caress, every smile had been an act designed to lull him into a false sense of security.

After she'd tipped him off, Fielding must have followed them and waited for his chance. It must have been a long evening, lurking in the darkness, waiting for exactly the right moment. A shot of them at the table at Gino's would have been much too tame, of course, Max thought grimly. So, he had waited until they walked across the beach, hoping they'd oblige with the perfect photograph.

He flung himself into his leather armchair and ran a hand across his eyes, groaning at the thought of Jack. He was about to disappoint him yet again. He had promised him that sailing trip, come hell or high water! Allegra was to have been invited, and Jack would be bitterly disappointed when he was told she wouldn't be going with them.

And much worse—tonight had probably sabotaged the plans he had to make the boy's presence in his home permanent.

Why was life so darned difficult without a partner to share it? There was no doubt about it—a wife would make all the difference. His mouth twisted. He wouldn't, after all, be going down that particular road! It would be a cold day in hell before he trusted any woman again, let alone married her!

He reached for the phone and dialed Ed's number. Better get him prepared for the morning tabloids!

It's been quite a night, Allegra told her tearstained image in the mirror. Betrayed by a man she thought of as a friend. Misjudged and condemned by the man she loved. Sad? Very! *So,* she asked herself fiercely, *what exactly do you intend to do about it?*

The answer came, very loud and clear. *Go home!*

Back to safety and sanity. Back to the comfort zone where she wasn't living each moment on a knife's edge. Back to a place where Max Tempest couldn't infiltrate.

So much, she thought with an ache, of her dreams of a new life in America. Perhaps this interlude with Max was a sign that she didn't belong here after all. Better, perhaps, to tread the familiar path than to stray into more dangerous waters. "Sorry, Dad," she whispered brokenly. "I thought I could make it over here. Looks like it's not meant to be, after all!"

Tomorrow she would drive to Tampa and get the first possible flight to London. Put the whole thing behind her. Pick up the threads of her life. Put thoughts of Max Tempest firmly behind her. The sooner, the better.

But first, she had one or two things to sort out.

She picked up the telephone and dialed for an outside line.

"For Pete's sake, Max! You know what time it is?" Ed groaned, his voice over the phone thick and blurred with sleep.

"Sorry, but it's important. Thought I'd better warn you before you see the morning papers."

"Oh, no!" Ed was instantly wide awake. "What now? I thought you were supposed to be staying out of trouble! How bad is it?"

"Could be worse. I've been set up. Paparazzi."

"Tell me you didn't kill anybody," Ed groaned.

"Sadly, no. He got away." Max's voice was laconic. He intended to keep his personal feelings strictly to himself. "But not before he took a nice little shot of me on a beach—with a lady."

"Who?"

"No one you know." He had no intention of mentioning Allegra's name.

"Well, thanks for the warning. What's done is done." Ed sighed. "Listen, have you made your mind up about the new contract? Time's running out if you want to make that sequel. I can't hold them off for much longer. They want you signing on the dotted line. Come on, Max! What's it to be? Your career—or that kid?"

Max frowned. "You'll be the first to know."

He replaced the receiver with a heavy heart. Tonight had begun so full of promise—with hope of real happiness. And now, the mere thought of Allegra Howard—the remembered scent and touch of her—filled him with despair.

As he went upstairs to his room, he felt utterly drained and bruised to the bone.

"I am so sorry, Miss Howard. Mr. Tempest, he is very busy." Maria's round face was red with embarrassment. "He will not see anyone today. He tell me not to disturb him!" Allegra's unexpected arrival had clearly thrown her.

"I'm sorry too, Maria. But this is very important."

Maria shook her head. "Please, no! He will be very angry!"

"Not with you," Allegra said. "I really must insist. Just for a few minutes."

She brushed past, ignoring the woman's protests, and headed to Max's study, Maria clucking at her heels.

Max had raised his head at the sharp rap on his door and stood, frozen to the spot, as Allegra flung herself into the room without waiting for an invitation.

For a few seconds they eyed each other in complete silence. Allegra, in a crisp white shirt and blue jeans, her hair in a severe chignon, was pale but utterly composed. And Max, rigid with shock, stared at her over the rims of his half-lens reading glasses.

"That's all right, Maria," he said at last and waited until, with curious eyes, she had closed the door behind her.

He put down the papers he was reading and threw the glasses on his desk. "What exactly do you want, Allegra?" His voice was a whiplash. "I told Maria I was not to be disturbed."

"So she said. Don't worry." Her hands were trembling as she dug into her bag. "This isn't a social call."

A second later and a tiny, flat object was hurtling across the room at him. His hand shot out instinctively to catch it.

"What's this?"

Allegra sighed. "What do you think it is? It's the memory card belonging to Rick Fielding's camera. And before you ask me what I had to do to get it, the answer's simple. I asked him for it. And because he owes me one, he had no choice but to hand it over."

Rick had sounded amazed, to say the least, when she had phoned him the previous night.

"You're joking! You? On the beach with Tempest?"

"Yes, me!" she'd snapped. "And spare me the wide-eyed innocence. You knew perfectly well who it was!"

But the amazement in Rick's voice had seemed genuine enough. "Believe it or not, I had no idea who it was. I thought it was some blond he'd picked up!"

"Oh, really?"

"It's the truth, I promise you! I never got a good look at your face." Then he'd laughed. "Well, if you play with fire, you get your fingers burned."

Allegra had ignored the barb. "Why did you want the photographs, anyway? I thought you were above that sort of thing?"

He laughed. "Just a little bit of mischief; let's just say I didn't like the way the guy looked at me the other night."

"I see. Well, I think it's time to call in the markers, Rick, don't you?"

He knew exactly what she meant. Allegra had once helped him out of a scrape, and there was no way he could refuse her request. If it hadn't been for her, he'd have been sacked soon after joining *Elegance* for failing to show up at an important photoshoot with a famous politician. Allegra had somehow managed to get a friend to stand in for him and had taken care that his boss hadn't found out about it. He'd never forgotten the kindness, and besides, Allegra was a colleague. He couldn't in good conscience refuse her request.

He groaned. "Okay," he muttered. "I'll get the films printed in the morning and get them over to you."

"Sorry, I need you to delete those photos, Rick." She didn't trust him an inch.

"Oh, come on! I promise not to do anything with them. I swear."

"Not good enough."

He groaned. "All right. I'll take care of it right now." Even the most unscrupulous hack observed a code of loyalty to one of his own.

Max was frowning, trying to make sense of what she was saying. "I don't understand . . ."

"It doesn't matter. All you need to know is that you're off the hook. As for your hang-ups and suspicions—you once said you were paranoid, and I think you were right."

"I didn't imagine Rick Fielding last night, Allegra. Or your connection with him."

Allegra's eyes were like chips of ice. "No, you didn't. But his presence on the beach had nothing to do with me. Rick didn't know it was me. In the darkness, I could have been anyone with blond hair. You see, he caught sight of you—quite by chance—driving that wreck of a car last night with a woman in the front seat—and like any good newspaperman, he knew he was on to a story."

Max looked unimpressed. "Do you really expect me to believe he didn't recognize you?"

"It's the truth. He actually slowed his car to let you pull out into the street. It was just a quick glimpse. He followed us but had some difficulty keeping up when you turned off at the beach, and he lost us. It took him a while before he finally spotted where you'd parked the car—and well, you know the rest."

Max's face remained impassive as Allegra went on relentlessly. "If you're not a newsman, I suppose it's hard to understand why anyone would want to take the photograph in the first place. It's not really Rick's field. But you didn't exactly endear yourself to him that night in the restaurant, and perhaps he was hoping to get his own back with something a bit racy for the tabloids."

Rick had more or less confessed that when he'd handed over the card . . .

"If it had been anyone else but you, I'd have had him," he'd growled. "And I hope the arrogant devil knows how lucky he is." She didn't intend repeating that, of course.

"Anyway," she went on, "I thought you might be grateful. At least you know your photograph won't be in the tabloids tomorrow."

"Just a minute." Max started toward her as she turned to open the door. "Do you really think you can walk out on me—just like that?"

She glanced at him coldly. "I have a plane to catch." She'd managed to get a cancellation on a flight to Gatwick.

One hand shot out to grab her arm, the other slamming the door shut before she could leave. "Don't be ridiculous!" He leaned, his hands on either side of the frame, trapping her. He was so close that she could see the tiny crescent-shaped scar at the corner of his mouth, feel the warmth of his breath on her cheek, sense the power emanating from his body.

"You're not going anywhere," he said, lifting one hand long enough to turn the key in the door and pocket it. "Not until you've convinced me you're telling the truth. That card could be blank for all I know!"

"What? You actually think I could be lying to you?" He wasn't just paranoid—he was downright offensive! The heat ran up into Allegra's face as she struggled to contain the powerful surge of outrage and hurt.

"I didn't say that! I just don't share your touching faith in your friend Rick."

"Oh, please! Why would he be crazy enough to try and trick me?"

"You tell me!" he snapped. "After that little performance on the beach last night, I guess I'm ready to believe anything!"

"Believe what you like!" She was determined not to show how much his words hurt her. "I don't care anymore what you think! So why don't you do us both a favor and unlock this door!"

Allegra was perilously close to losing her temper completely. The urge to lash out at him as he stood there, barring her way, was almost irresistible.

She took a deep, calming breath, digging her nails into the palms of her clenched hands.

"Do you really want me to shout for help and risk upsetting Jack?" she said, remembering that first day when she had been sorely tempted to push him into the swimming pool. She should have had the courage of her convictions—and saved herself a lot of hassle.

"Jack isn't here. He's out fishing with Carlos."

She gritted her teeth. "Maria, then."

He laughed grimly. "Deaf as a post, I'm afraid."

It was the way he went on standing there, calm and immobile, that finally sent her over the edge. "Open this door! At once!" She struck out, fiercely pounding the hard, unyielding wall of his chest with furious, impotent fists.

Max stood there calmly taking the blows, waiting for Allegra to spend herself, watching as strands of her glorious hair escaped her chignon and began to fall loosely around her hot face. Then, as her hands dropped to her sides, he stepped back, suddenly ashamed of himself. He should not have driven her to such lengths. He'd behaved like a fool, and now he wasn't sure what to do. He couldn't keep her here against her will any longer, but at the same time, he couldn't let her go like this. Not before he had apologized, taken back some of the things he had said so deliberately to anger her.

He had no idea what had driven him to go on goading her when it had been clear to him from the first that she had been speaking the simple truth. All he knew was that the sight and touch and scent of her as she stood, still his captive, with her back to the door, affected him so profoundly that he had to look away as he took the key from his pocket and held it out to her.

She snatched it from him, turning to the door, and as he looked down at her bent head and the sweet, vulnerable nape of her neck, his self-control snapped.

"Allegra, wait!"

She ignored him, her shaking hands fumbling as she tried to turn the key into the lock, and in sudden desperation he grabbed her, spinning her around to face him.

Then, as his hands burned through the thin cotton of her shirt, the atmosphere around them was suddenly charged with quite a different kind of electricity.

"Max, wait!"

"I've been waiting for you too long!" he said, his voice ragged.

He lifted his hand and ran his thumb over her mouth. "Don't say anything," he said softly. And then she stepped forward into the circle of his arms. He brushed her eyelids with his lips, moved softly down her cheek to the tender spot at the point of her chin.

And then he kissed her. As he held her in his arms, he knew he could not let her walk out of his life a second time. Knew that his world had been altered irrevocably by her sudden arrival into it. Knew that he would be crazy to let her go without telling her how much he loved and wanted her.

He looked down into her flushed face, stroked a strand of hair from her hot cheek, opened his mouth to tell her what was in his heart. And then his cell phone started ringing.

He groaned, tempted not to answer. But Carlos had taken Jack out in the boat. . . . As he hesitated, Allegra made his mind up for him.

"Answer it."

"Daria?" He sighed.

Allegra could hear the tone of the high, urgent, childish voice on the end of the phone, and as she backed away, Max put out a hand to deter her.

"Okay," he said. "Sure, I'll be there. Yes. In about an hour. No problem. Just stay put."

"I really must go," Allegra said politely in a bright, clear voice, as if she was about to take leave of her host at some social occasion.

"Don't run away!"

"I have to go."

"That was Daria. She's being discharged from the hospital. I guess she's still feeling a little shaky and there's no one else to pick her up."

Allegra nodded. "Then I'd better let you get on with it," she said, her wooden expression concealing the ache inside. She knew now how foolish she had been to imagine that she might have a place in Max's life. Nothing had changed from the time he had closed the door on that gauche seventeen-year-old shivering on his doorstep. Max might be attracted to her, might be fond of her, even. But there was always going to be someone more important than she was. Once it had been Annie. Then Jack. Now Daria. She would never come first with this man, and it was just as well she had finally realized it.

"I can't let you leave like this." He took her hands and held them against his chest, and she felt his heart beating strong and fast against her palm. "At least, let me explain to you how I feel."

She took her hands away and shook her head. "I think we've said it all, don't you?" she answered very quietly, and opened the door.

"This is it, then? You really are leaving? What can I do to make you stay?" He sounded utterly wretched. But, Allegra reminded herself furiously, he was, after all, a brilliant actor.

"At least," he said desperately, as she began to walk away from him, "let me take you back to the hotel."

"No, thanks. I have to return the boat I hired."

He stopped, shaking his head, the ghost of an ironic little smile lifting the corner of his beautiful mouth. "Yesterday," he said, "I was really beginning to believe I might be able to get it right."

Allegra didn't look back. That dejected note in his voice, that downcast look—a long time ago it might have worked its magic. But she wouldn't be falling for it. Not now. Not ever.

"Good-bye, Max." she said.

Afterward, her recollection of leaving the house and steering the boat back to Cedar Bay were hazy. All she could think of was getting as far away from Max as possible. Everything else was a blur. When, hot and shaking, she finally reached the hotel and the blessed privacy of her room, she rushed to the bathroom and leaned over the sink, splashing cold water over her burning face.

She wanted to weep over her lost hopes. But she wouldn't cry over Max. Never again. It was over. How could she ever have believed that they could be together? That was the stuff of dreams. Tomorrow she would be back in London, in the real world. And then she would be able to put the whole fantastic episode firmly behind her.

Max couldn't believe she'd actually gone. And worse, that he had merely stood by and let her leave. Only last night, on the beach, before they had been so brutally interrupted, he had been utterly convinced that Allegra's feelings truly matched his own. And today, he hadn't imagined her response when he had held her in his arms. A moment later and they would both have been confessing the truth about the way they felt about each other.

But it wasn't, somehow, meant to be. He'd blundered again and lost her just as he had before.

And right now, he had no idea what to do about it.

Chapter Twelve

Winter had come early, or so it seemed to Allegra as she hurried to the tube station at Waterloo on a chilly autumnal night. The car was packed as usual, and she had to straphang all the way to Clapham Junction before finally getting a seat and a chance to glance at the evening paper.

One look at the page in front of her seriously interrupted the normal rhythm of her heartbeat and drained her cheeks. Max! Here in London!

The grainy photograph didn't do him justice, of course. How could it? She would never forget the way he looked! The silver eyes, the glossy hair, and that enigmatic lift of one dark eyebrow were forever etched in her memory. When she dreamed about Max Tempest, it was always in color. And now, sitting there in her drab surroundings, damp and disheveled from the rush-hour scramble, Allegra saw him just as he was on that last day on Shell Island.

Helplessly, she devoured the brief article that accompanied the photograph, and her mouth curved into a smile.

Arriving at Heathrow to attend this evening's West End premiere of Tycoon, *his latest film, superstar Max Tempest was clearly in no mood for conversation!*

Typically, he was as tight-lipped as ever, refusing to comment on rumours that he is quitting Hollywood for good, having recently gained custody of his seven-year-old nephew, Jack. The star is renowned for his penchant for beautiful women. Now, he seems to be making an effort to put aside his bad boy image. Not before time!

So, he'd done it! Allegra smiled with genuine delight. Whatever her private feelings about Max, it was good news about Jack. The rest of it was the usual innuendo and speculation that characterized the gossip columns.

She closed the newspaper and stuffed it down the side of the seat. If she wasn't careful, she'd soon be ruining the months of self-talk—eliminating all thoughts of Max Tempest from her mind. After that painful last encounter in Florida, it was time to move on. Max might have been the one man in the world for her, but his presence in her life could only bring her unhappiness. Twice, he had quite deliberately forced her to acknowledge her feelings for him. And twice, when her defenses were down, he had just as deliberately rejected her. She could never let it happen again.

She'd been determined to be strong from the start, refusing to speak to him on the phone when he'd tried to contact her through *Elegance* and ignoring the letter he'd written her. The airmail envelope, with a return address in New York, lay crumpled and unopened at the bottom of her handbag. She carried it like a talisman, transferring it almost obsessively from bag to bag as if she still wanted to preserve her memories of Max. She couldn't bring herself to throw it away unread. At least, she had told herself, not yet. One day soon, she promised herself, she would be strong enough to do both.

At home, in the comfort of her flat, she turned on the central heating and played back her messages: Someone trying to sell her insurance. Her brother reminding her it was her stepfather's sixtieth birthday next week. An invitation from someone she'd met at a party asking her to dinner. Nothing special. She kicked off her shoes, walked across her elegant, minimalist living room to draw the curtains against the darkness.

It had stopped raining, but the yellow light from the streetlamps was reflected in dismal puddles on the pavement. A typical English scene, she found herself thinking bitterly, watching the traffic piling up in the street, and she suddenly longed for Florida sunshine and blue skies.

She closed the curtains with an angry little snap. For heaven's sake! All it took was one blurred photograph to undo all the good she had done. She'd thrown herself into her work after her return to London—had tried to step up her social activities, determinedly accepting invitations and partying with a kind of desperate enthusiasm that had never come easily to her. But life seemed to her increasingly humdrum, and she had, at the moment, no idea what to do about it.

The time she had spent with Max had definitely clouded her plans to look for a transfer to the States in the immediate future. One day, perhaps, she kept telling herself. But first, she needed breathing space, to recover.

Helena had been pleased with her article on Max, and it had come out in the October issue. Normally she enjoyed seeing her work in print, but somehow she hadn't been able to bring herself to read it. She now realized how wise she'd been. The mere sight of that photograph tonight had triggered unwelcome thoughts. Even so, she suddenly found herself wishing she hadn't left the newspaper in the train. She might have risked just one more glance. Where was Max staying? Probably in one of the Knightsbridge hotels favored by movie stars.

For heaven's sake, she told herself fiercely, *get a grip!* She reached for the remote and switched on the television, desperate for a diversion. Then she sat down quickly, as her legs suddenly threatened to give way under her.

On the screen, Max seemed larger than life as he stood in the foyer of Claridges, unwillingly submitting to the questions of a determined TV presenter.

"So, how hard was it for a single man like yourself to get custody of a seven-year-old?"

"He's my nephew," he said brusquely. "That helped."

"I hear he spent the summer with you in Florida?"

"That's right." He nodded. "And," he added with a wintry smile, "I guess that's all I have to say on the subject."

"Could you just tell us if it's true you've decided not to star in the sequel of *Tycoon*?"

"No comment."

"You realize your fans will be devastated?"

It was then, as he gave that characteristic grin just before his face disappeared from the screen, that the longing hit her with inexorable force.

The sudden, crazy desire to see him again in the flesh was so overwhelming that she had snatched up her coat and bag and slammed the door shut behind her before she had time to think it through. All she knew was that something outside common sense was driving her. It was illogical, preposterous, and utterly absurd, but she knew she had to see Max just one more time. All she needed was a brief glance. She'd make sure that he would have no idea that she was there, of course. And then, perhaps, she could finally put it all behind her and get on with her life.

Max stared out of the steamed-up window as the limousine glided through the wet London streets toward Leicester Square.

"This miserable weather," Ed muttered. "Does it ever stop raining here? And the traffic!" He groaned as they waited at the traffic lights behind a double-decker bus. "You have to admit, you can't beat wintering in L.A."

Max made no reply. If Ed thought he could persuade him to change his plans, he was wasting his time. His mind was made up, he thought, as they slowed down outside the Odeon, longing for this last meaningless showbiz ritual to be over.

As they moved toward the red carpet area where uniformed attendants waited to open the doors, Max took one look at the excited fans waving autograph books and craning their necks for a better look—at the barrage of press photographers waiting to pounce—and knew he had made the right decision. Enough was enough.

"For Pete's sake," Ed said urgently, as the car glided to a halt. "Smile!"

The adrenaline had been fairly surging through her veins as Allegra slipped through the mob of film fans awaiting the arrival of the stars. Somehow, she managed to work her way forward—just close enough to ensure a good view across the crush barriers.

An excited girl on her right smiled at her.

"I can't wait! Max will be here any second!"

Allegra smiled back, suddenly nervous. Was she standing too close for comfort? It was too late to draw back. The first of the black limousines was gliding to a halt only a feet away from her, and the doors were being opened.

The tall figure in formal evening dress emerged from the car with his back to her. But there was no mistaking the spare, elegant figure as he slid out of his seat to begin his walk across the red carpet with flashbulbs exploding around him. Allegra had been sure she was prepared for the sight of him, but the shock took her breath away, as her lips silently formed his name. He was close enough for her to have reached out and touched the fine broadcloth of his evening suit. She watched him turn to face the crowd of rapturous fans, saw him reach out to sign an autograph book, his smile a little strained but genuine enough.

Then, quite suddenly, one of the barriers gave way and toppled over—and the crowd surged forward. They poured through the gap, leaving Allegra standing there, exposed—in virtual isolation.

Max stood very still as the security men rushed into action to screen him from the unruly mob. And then, as if drawn by some mysterious force, he suddenly turned his head and met Allegra's eyes.

The effect was sudden and extraordinary. The world changed in a flash from monochrome to glorious Technicolor. For a second or two, seeing the look of intense pleasure on his face, Allegra felt her heart would burst. Even then, instinct told her to run, but somehow she couldn't make her legs work. It would have been futile, anyway, because, incredibly, Max was coming toward her. Ducking under the protecting arms of the security men, he moved with such speed that the crowd scarcely had time to realize what was happening. A few strides and he had reached one of the barriers and vaulted over it. Allegra gasped, almost staggering as he snatched her hand, and the next minute he was hauling her across the street, forcing her to match his stride. Somewhere behind she heard voices calling his name, but his pace never faltered. Together, they turned the corner of the street and as they ran down Charing Cross Road toward Trafalgar Square, Max hailed a passing cab and wrenched open the door. The next minute, Allegra, head spinning, found herself being flung headlong inside.

If the driver recognized one of the passengers breathing hard at the back of his cab, he made no comment. He merely grinned at them in his mirror.

"Where to, guv?"

"Anywhere. Just keep driving," Max said. "Do you know some place where we can have a little privacy?"

"In London? You must be joking, mate!" The cabbie laughed as he turned onto the Embankment. He pointed upward where the great wheel of the London Eye seemed to hang, suspended, above the city, a bright halo against the night sky. "You could try that! There's bound to be an empty capsule in this weather!"

"Great! Take us there!"

"Max! Are you out of your mind?" Allegra, still catching her breath, stared at him in bewilderment. "What on earth d'you think you're doing?"

He laughed and closed the glass partition behind the driver. "What I should have done years ago. Leaving it all behind."

"But the premiere . . ."

"Let me worry about that. There are far more important things to discuss."

Allegra, still trembling from shock and utter disbelief, stared at him blankly. "Such as?"

He turned to her in the darkness and captured one of her hands. "Such as why you wouldn't speak to me on the phone? Or at least answer my letter?"

"You know why." She clenched her jaw, determined to ignore what the warm pressure of his hand was doing to her breathing. "I can't afford to have someone like you in my life, Max. It's too . . . painful."

She might as well be completely honest—after all that had happened, what was the point of hiding her true feelings?

He raised an eyebrow. "Really? So, what were you doing standing there in the crowd tonight?"

"Perhaps," she said, removing her hand from his grasp, "I was hoping to convince myself once and for all that I was over you!"

"And are you?"

She shrunk back into the corner of the cab. "It doesn't matter. This is madness and you know it." It was incredibly difficult to be sitting there in that enclosed space, impossible not to react to the touch and scent and sight of him.

Evening clothes suited him so well, she found herself thinking distractedly. In her workaday raincoat with her hair hanging in damp ringlets after the mad scramble for the taxi, the contrast between them could not have been more marked. How could she ever have imagined she could cross the barriers between them and become part of his supercool world?

"Allegra," Max said softly, "that last day in Florida . . ."

"Let's pretend Florida never happened, shall we?" Her name on his lips had always reduced her to jelly, but her voice, hard and unrelenting, concealed it. "The whole thing was a mistake from the beginning. I shouldn't have agreed to do the interview. We were never meant to meet again. So let's just go our separate ways and call it quits."

"I don't believe I can do that."

"Sorry!" Her voice was harsh. "I'm afraid you'll have to!"

"Is that really what you want?"

Oh, she wouldn't be fooled by that pleading note in his voice! After all, she was dealing with a consummate actor!

"Yes," she snapped. "Absolutely."

"You can't deny a tourist a ride on the London Eye," Max said as the cab turned into Jubilee Gardens.

"Max!"

"There you go, mate." The cabbie pulled up to let them out close to the great circle of light. "That'll be a tenner." He beamed broadly at the size of the tip. "Thanks very much, guv." He winked. "And good luck to you!"

The girl at the ticket office took one look at them and smiled. She could spot romance a mile off. Such a stunning couple, all flushed and dewy-eyed. And didn't the bloke look sort of familiar?

"I don't suppose," she said, eyeing him appreciatively, "you'd fancy taking our private champagne flight? We've had a cancellation."

"Sounds good to me!"

Allegra tugged at his sleeve. "Max, no!"

He ignored her. "Indulge me. Just this once!"

Allegra felt giddy with a mixture of confusion and excitement as slowly, they glided upward into the night sky . . .

"This," she said shakily, "is crazy." But she couldn't suppress the feeling of anticipation as they soared higher and higher over the great city.

"I couldn't let you walk away from me until you at least heard me out," Max said, drawing her close. "I haven't spent all these months thinking about you to end up with another door slammed in my face. I have things I need to say to you."

"Such as?" Oh, Lord! Why wouldn't he stop looking at her like that?

"Such as I'm done with Hollywood. No more films."

"So what has that got to do with me?"

"Everything," he said. He moved toward her and touched her flushed face with gentle fingers. "Have you any idea," he asked her sternly, "how I feel about you?"

She recoiled from him as sharply as if he had struck her.

"No!" It wasn't an answer to his question—just one last, desperate attempt to keep him at bay.

She put out a hand blindly, almost as if to ward him off—a pitiful, hopeless gesture that wouldn't have convinced a fool. "Please, Max! It's not fair! Don't start all this again!"

He looked down into her face, and something he saw in the soft light must have confirmed what he had hoped for since the moment he had seen her standing in the crowd at the premiere.

"Be quiet," he said softly and caught her in his arms, lifting her off her feet, crushing her against him, kissing her until her body at last relaxed against him and her lips were on fire.

When he raised his head, they looked down together at the magnificent vista four hundred and fifty feet below. The whole city was a festival of lights spread out beneath them like some bejewelled tapestry—the Thames a glittering necklace studded with gems and the familiar landmarks, ancient and modern, bathed in radiance . . .

He took both her hands in his, pressing them to his lips. "Can't you understand? I love you. That last day, surely you knew how I felt? There was so much I wanted to say to you. And then Daria called. You never gave me a chance. I couldn't believe it when you just left without a word."

"I thought . . ." she began shakily.

"I don't care what you thought," he whispered against her throat, "I won't let you escape from me again."

Only then did she give herself up entirely to his embrace, all restraint melting away, coherent thoughts vanishing . . .

"I can't believe how much time we've wasted," he groaned. "You must admit—you gave me a hard time, sweetheart. From the first moment I discovered you breaking and entering!"

Allegra laid her head on his shoulder and stared, still dazzled by the view. "You shouldn't have pretended not to recognize me!"

"I needed the time to get myself together after the shock of seeing you after all those years." Max sighed. "I couldn't believe it was really you! And then complications set in. First, I managed to convince myself that you and Rick Fielding were out to nail me!"

Allegra grinned. "Then I decided to freak out about

poor Daria! I think I wanted to go on believing that you were a womanizer just to keep from admitting to myself how I felt."

"And then, when I finally thought we were about to move on, Rick Fielding managed to get in on the act." He held her closer. "It was crazy to doubt you. No wonder you ran away."

"Daria wanting you again was just the last straw! I just felt that there was no room for me in your life." Allegra had the grace to look ashamed. "How is she, anyway?"

"Fine. Her mother's taken her in hand, and they're back in London. I even thought of getting them to contact you on my behalf but then realized it might not help. Do you know," Max asked, "how hard I've tried to reach you? I did my best to charm your address and phone number out of those very formidable receptionists of yours, but they weren't having any."

Allegra grinned. The girls had been convinced he had been some weirdo pretending to be Max Tempest.

"Then, when you didn't answer my letter," he said, "I finally gave up trying to contact you. The only thing that kept me going was the knowledge that I'd be here in London for the premiere. I intended to pay your editor a personal visit."

Allegra laughed. "Believe me, she'd have fallen at your feet!" She looked at him shyly. "I should have had the courage to read your letter, shouldn't I?"

Max leaned back to look into her face. "You didn't even read it?" he asked incredulously.

"At the time, I was doing my best to forget you. But I

kept it with me, always." Her face burned. "Shall I read it now?"

"Why not?" There was an odd catch in his voice. "It won't take you long."

For some reason she could not quite fathom, Allegra's hands were shaking as she rummaged in her bag for the envelope, tore it open, and drew out the single sheet.

The letter consisted of just two words, and the bold black handwriting emphasized the urgency of the simple message: *Marry me!*

Allegra's eyes widened. The words had taken her breath away. She had been tempted so many times to open that envelope, but never in her wildest dreams had she imagined this.

"You really mean it?"

Max laughed brokenly. "If only I could make you understand how much I want you to be my wife." He bent to kiss her mouth, and they were on fire again. The mood had shifted, had become more intimate and more intense, every touch, every caress bonding them closer until at last Allegra found the words she had been so afraid to utter.

"I love you, Max."

"And you'll marry me—and take us on, Jack and I? I fly back home tomorrow to sign the legal papers. He's back in the foster home and I've been staying in New York to be near him. We leave for Wyoming next week." He grinned. "You can't really bring up a kid in the penthouse suite at the Waldorf-Astoria."

"Might be difficult!"

He brushed her forehead with his lips. "D'you think

you could get used to life in the mountains? If I promised you vacations on our favorite island?"

"Oh, Max," she said, "of course I could! I just can't believe this is really happening."

"A Christmas wedding," he said seriously, "in an English country church. It's time Jack and I met your family. And then back to Wyoming. You needn't give up your writing—you can just freelance."

Allegra sighed, happiness surging wildly inside her. She was going home at last—and with the man she loved.

"There's just one thing," he whispered against her lips as the rain stopped and a lone star emerged from behind a cloud. "I've never approved of only children. Have you?"

She shook her head, her eyes bright with joy.

"In that case," Max said as he gathered her into his arms, "we'd better get this wedding organized as soon as possible. We've wasted far too much time already."